An Impossible Life

David Black

An **Impossible Life**

⤶ A BOBEH MYSEH

A Novel

MOYER BELL

Wakefield, Rhode Island & London

Published by Moyer Bell

Portions of this book have appeared in different form in *Argonaut, Tikkun,* and *The Notre Dame Review.*

First Edition

LIBRARY OF CONGRESS CATALOGING-IN-PUBLICATION DATA

Black, David, 1945–
   An impossible life / by David Black. — 1st ed.
      p.   cm.
   ISBN 1-55921-222-5   (cloth)
   I.Title.
PS3552.L32A5   1998
813'.54—dc21   97-44877
                                                        CIP

Book design by Julia Sedykh

Printed in the United States of America.
Distributed in North America by Publishers Group West,
P.O. Box 8843, Emeryville, CA 94662,
800-788-3123 (in California 510-658-3453).

CHAPTER

 *one*

I

Frederick Binz—Binzy, the drummer in my father's old jazz band—visited my mother in the mental hospital on the first day of Passover.

He arrived about four in the afternoon, wearing a battered fedora—my mother called it his *Johnny Dollar* hat—a pale pink shirt with French cuffs held together by two-inch paper clips, and an orange sports coat with lime-green pinstripes making six-inch-wide checks. In 1944, in the Catskills, the outfit would have been sharp.

The nurses said he brought an accordion and spent the first hour of his visit playing "Broadway, My Street."

I can imagine him, running through the old Clayton-Jackson-Durante routine he and my father did in our living room almost forty years before when he came to Springfield, putting on a heavy Brooklyn accent, pronouncing *joint, jernt* . . .

I ordered hamburger à la carte, but I got a little dubious about the meat when the waiter asked me if I wanted it win, place, or show . . . *Stop the music, stop the music* . . . *Ah, Broadway* . . . *The sightseeing buses* . . . *old women sitting in them making believe they're customers. They're just decoys to draw trade* . . . *Broadway* . . . *It's a fake, it's a phony, but it's my street, the center of the world* . . . *Look who's coming down the street* . . . *Isn't he the well-dressed man. Tuxedo, high hat* . . . *He must be some big society fella* . . . *Wait a minute, his shirt's lighting up* . . . *He's advertising the Ice Palace, skating every night* . . . *Stop the music, stop the music* . . .

While my father accompanied him on the cornet, Binzy rolled a hat down his arm, cocked his head to one side, and strode stiff-legged across the rug . . . *Stop the music* . . .

Binzy spent the night. I was thrilled by the stories of jazz clubs and vaudeville, excited to imagine my father on a bandstand in a white dinner jacket, sweating as he played songs like the ones Binzy asked him to do that night: *Angeline, Hong Kong Blues, Just A Simple Melody, Ostrich Walk* . . .

Pulling my mother out of her chair, Binzy whirled her around the floor. My father looked down the length of his cornet at them.

Bea grabbed my hand and dragged me onto the rug, jitterbugging around me in a parody of my mother and Binzy, wagging her finger in the air, tossing her hair, kicking her legs out to the side . . . I shuffled in place.

When my father started playing *The Wha-Wha Blues*, my mother put the tips of her fingers against Binzy's chest, gently pushed him away, and, laughing, told him, "Enough."

"Ethel," Benzy begged.

My mother's face glistened, her eyes shone. Using one hand, she unclipped her earrings—plastic pearls the size of marbles—a dreamy gesture that embarrassed me. The gesture—I think now, remembering back—of a woman getting ready to make love.

Round-faced, whiskery, mouth red from sweet wine, Binzy looked like the Wyeth illustration of Friar Tuck in my copy of *Robin Hood*. I imagined him sneaking into Springfield to escape the Sheriff—which, in fact, he was doing. There was a warrant out for his arrest in Hartford, Connecticut, for kiting checks.

After dancing with my mother, Binzy pulled out a crisp linen handkerchief, blew his nose in it, and tossed it into a waste basket. He bought them two, three dozen at a time, and threw them out once he used them. It was the mark of a gentleman, he explained. And he asked me to get him a fresh handkerchief from his suitcase.

I climbed to the third floor, the small room at the top of the attic stairs, which already had his smell. Bay rum and cigars.

In his suitcase, I found a magazine. By today's standards it would seem quaint. Picture spreads about nudist colonies and Polynesian dancers. One photo showed a naked girl in some Los Angeles version of Tahiti daintily climbing down rocks beside a waterfall. Her head was lowered, watching the path, I guess.

One arm was extended for balance. She wore an orchid in her hair. I remember the flower in color, but I'm sure the picture was in black-and-white. One foot was in front of the other. At her crotch was a wisp of shadow, her pubic hair. I stole the magazine and hid it in my room.

When I went downstairs to deliver the handkerchief, Binzy tipped me a dollar. A fortune!

"Binzy!" My mother tried to take it from me to give it back.

"What are you going to buy with it, kid?" Binzy asked.

Ten comic books or twenty Skybars, licorice whips or caps for my Hopalong Cassidy pistol, X-ray glasses, which, according to the ad in the back pages of *EC Comics*, let you see a woman's breasts through her sweater . . .

I told Binzy I'd never had a dollar before.

My father stopped playing. He put his cornet back in its box, snapped the latches, and stowed the box in the front hall closet.

"I'm turning in," he said. Without waiting for anyone to answer, he climbed the stairs.

Binzy and my mother exchanged a look which I did not understand.

"What's wrong with Daddy?" Bea asked.

"I didn't mean to embarrass him," Binzy told my mother.

"Look, he doesn't even get an allowance," my mother said. She was talking about me. "How could you know?"

"Things are that tight?" Binzy asked.

My mother started to cry. She didn't even sit down. There was something terrible about her standing in the middle of the room, her hands hanging helplessly at her sides, crying . . .

"If I can help . . . ?" Binzy started.

"Upstairs," my mother turned to Bea, to me. "Both of you."

As Bea and I climbed to the second floor, I asked why Mom was so sad.

"Don't be so stupid," Bea said.

She went into her room and closed the door.

I heard my father in the bathroom. He was standing at the sink, in his pale blue pajama bottoms, brushing his teeth. He glanced at me, his mouth all foamy, the toothbrush sticking out like a cigar.

"I love you, Dad," I said.

He stared at me for a long time. Then, taking the toothbrush from his mouth, but not wiping away the foam, he said, "When you're grown up, no matter what happens, don't ever, ever forget to brush before you go to bed."

Then he closed the bathroom door.

Downstairs, I heard Mom locking up. Binzy was half-humming, half-singing, *Oh, Miss Hannah*. Then, he stopped. There was a silence.

I stood at the top of the stairs and looked down into the front hall, where Binzy was kissing my mother . . . A long kiss.

My mother coyly turned her head and raised one shoulder—birdlike—as Binzy started up the stairs. I stepped back, but not in time. Binzy saw me.

The bathroom door opened. My mother—now, she was humming, *Oh, Miss Hannah*—started up the stairs. Binzy reached the top and put his hand on my shoulder. My father came out of the bathroom—and looked at Binzy and me, standing there.

"You got a good boy here, Abe," Binzy said.

And he tightened his grip on my shoulder just enough to hurt.

The next morning, when I came down for breakfast, Binzy asked if I'd take his suitcase down to his car. As I was leaving the room, he said, "Do me a favor. Check and make sure I didn't leave anything behind."

When I slipped Binzy's magazine back into his suitcase, I put the dollar he'd given me in, too.

Binzy jumped into his car, hit the starter button, and put the car in gear, backing out of the driveway and our lives, with a roar.

Stop the music!

II

By the time I arrived at the hospital, Binzy was no longer performing. He sat stroking my mother's hand. When I entered the room and introduced myself, he said, "You look like your father. Ethel, doesn't he look like Abe?"

My mother blinked at me with watery eyes. Her mouth was half open, and her tongue explored a cold sore on her lip.

"Do you know who I am?" I asked.

"You look just like my son," she said.

"I am your son," I said.

She looked at Binzy.

"Leo's here," she said.

"The year she met your father," Binzy said, "she was dating a gangster named Larry Ascot."

Larry Ascot, whose real name was Morris Rubin, ran the gambling action in Providence for the mob in New York, according to the few newspaper clips I dug up on him. The first clip, from *The Providence Journal*, no date, probably spring, 1937, is sketchy. A mention that he had come to town to attend an opera benefit, *Otello*. The benefit coincided with some trouble at Narragansett Park, the race track. A jockey named Rabbit O'Dwyer was found drugged and tied to a chair in the stables with his eyelids cut off.

"That's okay," someone on the street told the cops. "After what he did, he's never going to get a wink of sleep anyway."

About a year later, the *New York Mirror* ran a photograph of Ascot. A tall man in a light-colored overcoat and opera scarf. His tie has a big knot that pushes up one wing of his shirt collar. He's grinning and pointing at the camera. Next to him is a man who stands no higher than his shoulder, wearing a coat that hangs to his ankles: Little Augie Neubetter, a *shtarke* from the Brownsville gang, who, along with Abe "Kid Twist" Reles, "Bugsy" Goldstein, and Harry "Pittsburgh Phil" Strauss, muscled in on the Brooklyn pinball racket controlled by the Shapiro brothers.

Neubetter was famous. In the early '30s, he'd walked up to a man in the lobby of the Half Moon Hotel in Coney Island and bitten off his nose. Neither Neubetter nor his victim ever explained why.

Two weeks after the item in the *Mirror*, Neubetter was found with his hat nailed to his head with a six-inch spike. One gang history explained that he had failed to take his hat off in the presence of a woman who'd been dating Ascot.

There's a six-year gap in the clips I was able to find. Monday, September 11, 1944. *The New York Daily News*. Page 1: *U.S. Big Guns Shell Reich*. Page 9: *The Inquiring Fotographer* asks, "What is a woman's greatest problem in life?" Marion Coddington Davis, Bayside Drive, school-girl, age sixteen, says: "Getting a good education and being popular, but yet retaining a good reputation." Page 11: Venus Ramey of Washington, D.C., poses with her crown and scepter, 1944's "Miss America," the first redhead to win the title. Page 13: *Broadway* by Danton Walker re-ported that bobby sox fans are swooning over a new crooner, Freddie Stewart. Walker also reported, "Internal revenue experts are now on the trail of known racketeers and so-called 'labor executives' who have found a haven in Los Angeles." And: "Hats off to Phyllis Berlin, a popular Conover model, who has returned Larry Ascot's ring . . ." Page 20: "Barnman Charlie Sheehan is the victim of the mysterious fire that destroyed sixteen thoroughbreds in Jay Howland's stable." Two weeks later Phyllis Berlin and Jay Howland were photographed coming out of the review *Good Girls Don't*. No one made the connection between the fire that destroyed Howland's stable and Howland dating Ascot's girl.

On Sunday, February 3, 1945, Bostonians could see a double-bill—Merle Oberon and Laurence Olivier in *Wuthering Heights* and Jack Benny in *Charley's Aunt*—at the Exeter. Deanna Durbin starred in her first Technicolor feature, *Can't Help Singing*. Symphony Hall was advertising Jose Iturbi. The Old Howard Burlesque was featuring

Lili Dawn, Hap Hyatt, Gloria Love, and Lou Devine. And Larry Ascot escorted an unknown brunette beauty to the Colonial Theater, where Tallulah Bankhead was starring in Philip Barry's new play, *Foolish Notion*.

The unknown brunette beauty was my mother.

Stop the music!

III

"On the side, Ascot lent money to Brown undergrads," Binzy said, "rich kids who couldn't get an advance on their allowance. Kids who got in over their head, gambling, whoring, whatever. These kids, they thought they were swift, leaving school, owing Ascot. What's he going to do? Chase them to Cleveland, Chicago, New York, and squeal to their daddies? Ascot didn't care. These kids grew up to be lawyers, judges, bankers . . . They owned, say, restaurants that maybe needed a new laundry service. Ascot was there with the suggestion they use his friend's. Or they became doctors. And maybe Ascot had an associate who knocked up a gal who needed an abortion. But your mother . . . All she saw was a guy in a white silk scarf."

Ascot lived in a suite at the Biltmore Hotel. He took my mother to the hotel's Baccante Room, where the waitresses wore short translucent skirts, to the Lafayette on the Boston Post Road, and gin mills on the way to Pawtuxet.

My grandfather, Sam, ran a grocery store. He'd be up at 4 A.M., getting ready to go to the markets to buy produce, fish, and meat, when Ascot's big yellow car would drop my mother off at my grandfather's house on Congress Avenue.

One morning in March, my grandfather appeared on the porch, a big man, as tall as Ascot, but broader, in suspenders and shirtsleeves with his derby on his head and holding a brimful glass of fresh-squeezed orange juice, which he carried out to the car.

Assuming the juice was for her, my mother reached for it, when my grandfather told her, "Go inside and wash your face."

My mother looked from her date to her father, went inside, and stood in the parlor, peeking out at the street through the curtains.

My grandfather handed the juice through the window to Ascot, who drank it without taking his eyes off my grandfather.

"You want corn flakes?" my grandfather said. "Matzoh-brai?"

"I haven't had matzoh-brai since I was a kid," Ascot said.

"Come," my grandfather said—according to Binzy.

Ascot got out of the car and followed my grandfather up the path to the house, two brawny men, squinting in the low early morning sun, a *shtetl* peasant and the son of a *shtetl* peasant, both a long way from the world that produced them. Ascot carried the now empty juice glass as carefully as my grandfather had carried the full glass. My mother fled into her bedroom—keeping the door cracked open.

"What happened?" I asked Binzy.

"They had matzoh-brai," Binzy said.

IV

My grandfather wasn't a religious man. He rarely went to Sabbath services, only occasionally to High Holy Day services. But, on weekdays, after going to the market, he went to a schul in the slums to help make up a minyan. At his urging, Ascot began going to services with him.

That spring, Ascot would drop my mother off around dawn, have breakfast with my grandfather, take a nap on the living room couch—while, thirty feet away, my mother lay sleepless in her bed, angry and puzzled. When my grandfather had finished marketing, he'd stop by the house and wake Ascot, who'd drive them to schul in his fancy car. After the service, Ascot dropped my grandfather at his store on Westminster Avenue, where my grandfather's brother Frank was already at work.

By late April, Ascot was hanging around the grocery store. His father had been a butcher; and my grandfather watched as Ascot, a bloody apron over his expensive shirt and suit pants, neatly trimmed the fat from a steak or chopped ribs.

At the end of the day, he'd help my grandfather scrub the butcher block with alcohol and light the sterilizing fire that burned with a glassy blue flame as they shared shots of schnapps.

Then, coats slung over their shoulders, they walked home, eating russet apples or slivers of Herkermer cheese.

The war, which made people reckless, was a bonanza for racing. In 1944, the seventeen states that allowed racing reported total legal bets of $1,126,308,645. The illegal bets were probably double that. Former Supreme Court Judge James F. Byrnes, the head of the Office of War Mobilization and Reconversion, had closed the race tracks on January 3, 1945. Ascot bet my grandfather the ban would be lifted before the beginning of June.

"I don't bet," my grandfather said. "On anything."

"Don't you want a little excitement in your life?" Ascot asked.

They were sitting at the kitchen table, eating corn flakes and drinking SweeTouchNee Tea.

My grandfather said, "Before I left home"—he meant Plissa, the town where he grew up in Lithuania—"I had enough excitement."

He stood up and, stripping off his shirt, showed the scars on his back, pale parallel stripes, where he'd been horsewhipped by Cossacks.

Without a word, Ascot stripped off *his* shirt, showing off a scar on *his* chest, where he'd been knifed in a brawl.

My grandfather pointed to a scar on his side, where, when he first came to Providence, another peddler had gashed him with a meat hook in a quarrel over turf.

Ascot unbuttoned his pants and showed a scar along his right thigh made by a rival gangster with a bottle of sulfuric acid.

My grandfather took a carving knife from a drawer and cut his left arm.

Ascot took the knife and cut *his* left arm.

By the time my grandmother came into the kitchen half an hour later, both men, standing naked in the middle of the floor, were bleeding from half a dozen self-inflicted wounds.

V

That was the last time Ascot came to the house—until my mother and father were married. My mother waited for him to call, to write; but he didn't.

She called his hotel and left messages, which he didn't answer. She went to the hotel and waited in the lobby, but she never saw him.

In May, when the ban on racing was lifted—as Ascot had predicted—my mother drove out to Narragansett Park and tried unsuccessfully to see him in his box. When she called to him, he ignored her.

Late in June, 1945, she tracked him down in a roadhouse, the Jug End—which, Binzy claimed, had been a Nazi-American youth hall before the war, Jug End being a corruption of *Jungen*.

My mother stood in the doorway, as Ascot danced with a blond in a peach-colored satin dress to *Feet Draggin' Blues*, the Harry James song, played by *The Bostonians*, my father's band.

"A dozen dames were watching Abe, all ga-ga," Binzy said.

While Binzy did some fancy stuff on the drums, my father conducted by waving his cornet and flirted with the girls crowding the bandstand.

When the song ended, my mother walked up to the

band and, as Ascot watched, gave my surprised father, the hero of the moment, a kiss.

"That's how they met?" I asked Binzy.

"All your father had to know was that he had a chance to go out with a gangster's girl," Binzy said.

"But, by then, she wasn't," I said.

"No," Binzy agreed, patting my mother's hand as she dozed in the hospital bed.

Quietly, he started humming *Oh, Miss Hannah.*

My mother opened her eyes, blinked at him, and said, "When you go, don't forget to turn out the lights."

Stop the music . . .

 *two*

I

I first realized my mother had become insane when she told me she had sifted my father's ashes through my sister's marijuana strainer into the garbage disposal. She was—she explained—looking for his gold fillings.

Q. Do you remember that photograph of your mother and me at Scarborough?

A. You're both lying on a blanket on the beach.

Q. Our first date. I drove down from Boston. She drove over from Providence. She wore a black knit bathing suit with an attached skirt that looked like a clown's ruff.

A. Modest.

Q. Risqué, back then.

A. Her hair was long.

Q. She never wore it that long after we were married.

A. In the photograph, she was squinting.

Q. Binzy had a Kodak. He shouted, "Look sharp." The sun was over his right shoulder and glared in our eyes.

A. It was before you knocked her up?

Q. What kind of talk is that?

A. Before you died, you told me she was two months pregnant with Bea when you got married.

Q. That's why we didn't have a synagogue ceremony. Just us, Larry Ascot, Grandpa and Grandma, and your Aunt Faye and Uncle Phil, who were both in uniform.

A. Faye was in the WACs?

Q. The WAVEs.

A. I remember *that* photograph. She looked like one of the Andrews Sisters.

Q. Phil looked like a sharpie.

A. With his pencil mustache.

Q. And Brylcreamed hair.

A. Binzy . . .

Q. Frederick Binz.

A. The guy with all the hookers.

Q. Where you get the dirty mouth?

A. When did you become a prude?

Q. You mean, regret my mistakes? I let you run wild.

A. You wanted Bea and me to be rebels.

Q. So she takes twenty years to finish college.

A. And I became a conservative.

Q. Thank God I died before *that* happened.

A. You said, when your band played the Catskills, every Sunday night, after you got paid for the week, your drummer—

Q. Binzy.

A. —would go to Katz's American Hotel—

Q. When did I tell you that?

A. —where there was a whorehouse.

Q. In the rooms behind the kitchen. I went with him a couple of times. Tiny rooms, the size of closets. Each one had a metal army cot, a small table, two chairs, and a galvanized metal sink. It was August. Moths batted against the screens—and left cream-colored powder from their wings in the wire mesh. The breeze smelled of citronella from the bug candles. And you could hear the sounds from the other rooms, where the townies were with their whores. The hotel guests, I don't think they knew about what was going on. It was a classy hotel. The napkins in the big dining room were linen and had the hotel monogram. Danny Kaye played there when he was just getting started. We used to kid Binzy about going to the whores. There were all these girls and mamas on vacation who were gaga for musicians.

A. But he said they were too much trouble.

Q. *Tsuris.* You've become a real goy. You remember what I said, but not how I said it.

A. You wanted me to be a goy.

Q. I wanted you to be . . . A success. To fit in. To have *polish*.

A. Polish?

Q. I can't remember.

A. You don't want to remember that. But you remember the gaga mamas and their gaga daughters.

Q. With them, after, you had to make conversation.

And, while you were doing your set, they'd look at you with bedroom eyes. In the break, they expected you to sit with them.

A. Even the married women.

Q. The husbands were all in the city, working.

A. Or they were too tired.

Q. You remember everything.

A. I can't tell what's remembered and what I've filled in later.

Q. You met Binzy once. When you were twelve or thirteen. He arrived in a '33 maroon Pontiac sedan. He had two women with him. A vaudeville act he was flogging on the Orpheum circuit, he said. A duet, he said. On the vibes. But they were strippers. They were doing a Rotary club in Agawam. So Binzy figured, half an hour away, why not stop by.

A. I don't remember the strippers. I remember Binzy spent the night. On the lam. From the cops in Hartford.

Q. Two nights.

A. I only remember one.

Q. And I don't remember the cops in Hartford.

A. And the strippers?

Q. Stayed at a hotel.

A. Binzy sang a Jimmy Durante song. And gave me a dollar.

Q. Five dollars.

A. Why do I remember only one?

Q. One was embarrassing enough for me. Mom made coffee and cinnamon toast.

A. Wait a minute. I *do* remember the strippers.

Q. You sound surprised.

A. No, I really do. One of the women smelled like the bushes we had out back, like lilac. She wore a green dress that shimmered in the electric light.

Q. You remember better than I do.

A. She was a stripper?

Q. And probably a hooker.

A. I used to dream about her.

Q. I'll bet lots of guys did.

A. Not that kind of dream. Something to do with the smell. The lilacs. And a cottage like the one we stayed in on Cape Cod when I was . . . I must have been nine. Maybe eight.

Q. Gloucester.

A. There was a penny candy store, where I bought strips of paper like adding machine tape that had different colored buttons made of sugar. You'd peel them off—or pry them off with your teeth . . . They always came away with a little of the paper.

Q. That was in Rockport. What about the stripper?

A. I went into the kitchen to get a drink of water or something . . . And she was standing in front of the refrigerator with the door open.

"Can I get you anything?" I asked.

Q. You remember the exact words?

A. No. But close enough.

She said, "No."

I waited.

She must have realized she needed to explain. So she finally said—and she sounded almost awe-struck—"You have so much food."

Q. She probably grew up hungry.

A. She wasn't much older than I was. Eighteen at the most.

Q. Binzy always liked his whores young.

A. The ones in the Catskills . . . ?

Q. Jewish girls who lived in cottages out by Monticello. They were driven to the hotel every night in an old yellow school bus. The one I went with—this was before your mother—had come originally from the Hassidic community there. You'd see the Hassids in their wide-brimmed hats and black wool coats in eighty-degree heat.

A. The Hassids' coats . . . When I was a kid, the wool was so nappy, it reminded me of one of my stuffed animals. A panda.

Q. Their women shaved their heads and wore wigs. The girl I was with, she left because she wanted to keep her hair.

A. You told me she had a crank record player.

Q. A Victrola. She played an old Brunswick of Ethel Waters singing *I Can't Give You Anything But Love*. Over and over.

A. Was that supposed to be a comment on what she was doing?

Q. A terrific record. Duke Ellington, Sonny Greer, Cootie Williams . . . I can't believe I told you that.

A. The day after your funeral, I found a bottle of phenobarbital in Mom's wastebasket.

Q. I used to make her take the pills. I knew, once I was gone, she'd stop.

A. So she was always crazy?

Q. Binzy warned me. After being with her that first night in Scarborough, he said, it's like she's on bennies.

A. The shrinks say she's a paranoid schizophrenic.

Q. They used to say manic-depressive.

A. She's convinced Maxie's father is part of a CIA conspiracy to turn Jews into Christians . . .

Q. Well, you marry a goy . . .

A. She's threatened to kidnap Rebecca to save her from being brainwashed.

Q. Threatened?

A. Every day, she writes thirty, forty-page letters . . .

Q. To you?

A. And Maxie. And Maxie's parents. And to every editor I've ever worked with. After I published a piece in the *Times Magazine*, she wrote over a hundred pages, documenting my father-in-law's conspiracy—and drove in from Springfield to deliver it to the *Times*, Abe Rosenthal, in person. The guard patiently listened to her cockamamie story, then told her she had a scoop but the wrong paper. He gave her the address of the *New York Post*.

Q. How old is Rebecca?

A. Five. The same age Mom was when her mother died. She said no one told her. Suddenly, her mother was gone; then, suddenly, she had a new mother . . .

Q. Your Grandma.

A. I didn't even know she wasn't my real grandmother until I was in eleventh grade. When I got home from school one afternoon, Mom sat me down beside her on the couch in the living room . . . Very formal. She even made us cups of tea with milk.

Q. She called that Scottish tea.

A. Why?

Q. Who knows?

A. And she started, *You know how some children are raised by people who aren't their parents?* I felt . . .

stagefright. Scared and excited. I loved the idea that I was an orphan, that you and Mom had adopted me, that my real parents were strangers.

Q. What was wrong with us?

A. You seemed ordinary.

Q. I was the son of a bootlegger. I killed a man when I was a teenager. He was threatening my father with a gun. I came into the kitchen of our apartment in Roxbury, grabbed him around the neck, and stabbed him in the chest with a carving knife. Ordinary?

A. You never told me that.

Q. Half a dozen times, I told you. You don't want to know, because—

A. Because what?

Q. Because you've become what I wanted you to be: more cultured than I was.

A. You spoke twelve languages. You could quote pages of Shakespeare. I can't do that.

Q. I had more to prove than you do. So what happened that afternoon with Mom?

A. A let-down. She explained Grandma was Grandpa's second wife.

Q. So much for your mysterious heritage.

A. Did you ever kill anyone else?

Q. It's not enough I was a dead-end kid who learned Greek, Latin, Middle-High German, Sanskrit . . . It takes murder to make me interesting? Let me ask you . . . Have you ever killed anyone?

A. No.

Q. In Vietnam?

A. I was a draft-dodger.

Q. You're proud I killed. I'm proud you didn't. Your mother must have been very ashamed of having a step-mother. She told me about Grandma the same time she told you.

A. By then, you'd been married seventeen years!

Q. So what are you going to do?

A. That's what I conjured you up to ask.

Q. I figured you needed my help for something. Almost a year dead, and you don't pray to me once.

A. Dad, you were an atheist. You brought me up to be an atheist.

Q. So why are you praying?

A. What *do* I do?

II

My mother explained that she had sifted my father's ashes because, on *Donahue*, she'd heard a funeral director esti-mate the millions of dollars in gold buried every year.

My ex-wife, Maxie, said that when I heard what my mother had done, I looked as if I was about to leap across the table and strangle her. I left dinner and sat on the edge of the tub in the downstairs bathroom. New chrome, bright tiles.

Maxie came into the little room, which had been a pantry before it had been transformed the year of my father's death, the year he finally had a little money to spend after two decades of scraping by on a high school English teacher's salary.

He'd been picked to be coordinator of English curriculum for the Springfield, Massachusetts, school system—an ambiguous honor. The city had been trying to get rid of him ever since the mid-fifties, the height of the McCarthy Era, when he'd been an outspoken socialist and union organizer.

But he was a Trotskyist and more anti-Soviet than J. Edgar Hoover. He believed Lenin betrayed the Revolution. So the House Un-American Affairs Committee—and its little brother in the municipal government—wasn't able to purge him.

For the next fifteen years, he continued to subvert his students by having them read *Rabbit, Run* and the un-bowdlerized version of *Romeo and Juliet*. Since the school committee couldn't get him out of the classroom by firing him, they did it by giving him a promotion.

With his raise, he built the bathroom, bought himself a gray pinstripe suit, an expensive briefcase, a stereo system, and a recording of Mahler's 2nd Symphony.

When I called him from New York, where Maxie and I had recently moved, he told me that he was being taken to lunch by the Prentice-Hall textbook rep.

"My first *expense-account* lunch," he said. "I think capitalists have more fun than socialists."

The morning of the lunch, he woke an hour earlier than usual, dressed in his new suit, packed his new briefcase, and sat in a straight-back chair in the middle of the living room wearing his new earphones and listening to his new recording of Mahler on his new stereo—which is how my mother found him, dead.

She took off the Mahler and put on Paul Robeson singing *Song of the Volga Boatmen*—an old 78. The new stereo played only 33 1/3s and 45s. When my sister, Bea—who lived outside of Amherst—stopped by an hour later, she found my father, still in the chair, listing thirty degrees off plumb, my mother in the kitchen, weeping as she folded laundry, and the Paul Robeson 78 playing at 33 1/3, even deeper and more lugubrious than ever.

Upstairs, outside the room my father used as a study, was a stack of books: *Friday Night Stories*, published by the Woman's League of the United Synagogues of America, *Ben Hur, Yankee Ships in Pirate Waters, Practical Bridge, Flotsam*, a novel by a turn-of-the-century writer named Henry Seton Merriman, *"Left-Wing" Communism, an Infantile Disorder* in a Little Lenin Library edition, two books by H. Allen Smith, Joe DiMaggio's autobiography, *Lucky to Be a Yankee*, and *Women in Prison*, a lurid paperback from the early fifties. When I was eleven, I used to study the picture of three female cons, whose crime seemed to be they looked easily-aroused.

There were also twenty-five stereopticon slides, *tableaux vivants*, telling the story of Jesus from *The Nativity* (slide number one) to *The Resurrection* and *The Ascension* (slides seventeen and eighteen). The remaining seven were photographs of sacred sites in the Holy Land when the slides were made in the late 1880s. I have no idea where my father got them. Or why.

The books and slides were all my mother wanted to save of my father's belongings.

Not knowing what else to do, Bea called the Rabbi of the Reform synagogue, who, when she told him what happened, said only, "I knew he'd come 'round," meaning that he always expected my father to shed his atheism on his deathbed.

"He didn't," Bea said. "I have."

The Rabbi—a plump man who wore expensive blue suits and whose flesh was as grainy as marzipan—Snyder, I can't recall his first name, arrived at the house an hour later and helped Bea make arrangements.

By the time Maxie and I got to Springfield, the next afternoon, all that remained of my father was in an urn in a box about a foot square wrapped in gold and black paper like a birthday present.

Q. Why the rush?

A. Bea said Mom wanted to do it—

Q. *Do it?* Do what?

A. The cremation.

Q. *Do it* . . . It sounds like sex.

A. —immediately. And Mom said *Bea* wanted to do it immediately.

Q. Probably the only time they ever agreed on anything.

A. Bea didn't want to believe Mom was crazy.

Q. Because Bea wanted to hate your mother. If Ethel was crazy, she'd have to forgive her.

A. Mom wouldn't let Bea's boyfriend in the house for the wake.

Q. Pineapple upside-down cake?

A. At the wake? Of course . . .

Q. What else?

A. Kugel. Macaroni and cheese. Tuna casserole. Bagels, lox, and cream cheese.

Q. When we first came to Springfield, there was only one place to get bagels.

A. Why did you move to Springfield?

Q. The *Springfield Plan* . . . It was one of the first attempts to legislate public school integration. The city was filled with Lefties. Lots of CP members. After their parents were executed, the Rosenberg kids lived there. . . .

A. One afternoon, when I was in tenth grade, I came home from school through Forest Park. It was five-thirty, six o'clock, already dark. I saw what I thought was a cookout. People around a campfire. When I got closer I saw a man with a noose around his neck, hanging from a tree. He was black. The men around the fire were, of course, all white. Some of them were parents of kids I went to school with. One of them turned and saw me on the edge of the firelight. He knew I knew him. I ran the rest of the way home.

Q. Who was the guy who saw you?

A. I guess it's the way God puns—his name was Lynch.

Q. From the library.

A. Weeks later, when I returned some books, he was at the check-out counter.

Q. Did he say anything?

A. No.

Q. Did you?

A. No. Last year, I used the incident in a script for a television show I wrote and produced.

Q. So you've become a big shot.

A. Every day, I miss you. But, if you were still alive, you probably would have ended up on the set, schmoozing with the grips, flirting with the actresses . . .

Q. I'd be almost eighty-five.

A. Like Harpo Marx. Chasing broads, honking your horn . . .

Q. You didn't like me.

A. I didn't know you. If we'd had twenty more years . . .

Q. You don't think it would be any different?

A. No.

Q. So . . .

A. Anyway, it was my first time producing. I was on the set when the actor told the lynching story, which in the script happened to him. I wasn't prepared for my reaction. I had to leave the room. It had been a fourteen, fifteen-hour day. Our location was in a poor part of Acapulco. Grips, actors, extras were hanging around outside in the street, exhausted. I went into my trailer, lay down, and couldn't breathe.

Q. Did people know it was a true story?

A. I made a joke about it . . .

Q. You always used to joke about serious things.

A. To keep me from getting serious about them. I learned it from you.

Q. I never joked about racism, politics, serious things.

A. You joked about your marriage, us kids. . . . You joked about my voice changing, my getting pubic hair, the first time I had to shave—

Q. Those things weren't serious.

A. You certainly never took them seriously.

Q. Stuff like that . . . Hey, I joked about myself, my limp, my wall eye, my father sticking me in an orphanage when I was a kid . . .

A. That's what I mean. To keep them from hurting.

Q. They hurt.

III

I arrived at the Medical Center General Hospital in Cranston, Rhode Island, the state asylum, before lunch. The police had called me about nine that morning to tell me my mother had been temporarily committed by the courts for observation.

She had started a fire in the middle of the living room of her beach-front apartment in Westerly, Rhode Island. Her landlady called the cops. They pounded on her door. She refused to let them in. She had only one window open, a narrow crack. From the street the flames flickering through that window looked like a red curtain blown out of the apartment by a breeze.

When the cops finally broke down the door and put out the blaze, my mother explained her reluctance to let them in by saying she was getting rid of evidence. Evidence of what? She refused to tell. Evidence of her life, I suppose.

The walls were covered—every square inch that hadn't been scorched by the fire—with minuscule handwriting, my mother's, a helter-skelter account of my father's death, my ex-father-in-law's conspiracy, magical incantations for exorcising Maxie from my life, tiny perfect drawings of things she must have seen around Westerly: a drugstore window-display with a row of old-fashioned apothecary jars, a man standing at the edge of the ocean, his trousers rolled around his calves, a gull picking at a periwinkle . . . I never knew my mother could draw.

When I went to the apartment to pay for the damages and to gather my mother's few belongings—only two suitcases worth, all she wanted to keep from the sixty-three years she'd been alive—walking into that room was like entering my mother's brain.

She had moved to Westerly about a month after she'd told me what she'd done with my father's ashes. All her life, she had wanted to live by the sea. Freed by my father's death from any restraints, she threw out everything— except the two suitcases, one full of clothes, the other full of books, papers, a few photographs, and two letters my father had written when he was courting her—sold the house for $10,000 less than she could have gotten if she hadn't been so desperate to escape from her past, from *our* past, *our* family; and drove to Rhode Island.

One of the things I retrieved from her apartment was a picture, apparently taken by a sidewalk photographer on a windy day, of my mother in a navy dress with a pattern of huge, twelve-inch, red blossoms, standing, one hand clapped to the crown of a new be-ribboned straw hat, the other extended in a comic vamping 1920s bathing beauty gesture. On the back of the picture, she had scrawled: *Me, the first day of my new life!*

Such hope. But her handwriting was shaky and disordered, already betraying the psychotic break to come.

Her raids on New York—on my family, my daughter— became frequent enough for me to call Bank Street, where my daughter went to pre-school, and warn them. The school psychiatrist had us tell Rebecca that she should scream and run if her Grannie tried to take her from the building.

"Is Grannie bad?" Rebecca asked.

"She's sick," Maxie said. "Her feelings are sick."

"Why do I have to run?" Rebecca asked. "Is it catching?" I was asking myself that, too.

"In the mental ward, maybe we should book a whole wing?" I said to Maxie that night after Rebecca had gone to bed. "Do you think they have family discounts?"

The grounds of the state hospital looked like a college campus. Three-story red brick buildings set in expansive lawns. My mother was in the violent ward. On the ceiling were sixty-watt bulbs in green-painted cages. The walls were the same green, chalkboard green. It was supposed to have a calming effect. The floor reeked of disinfectant. I followed an aid as she unlocked one barred door after another.

She went to get Mom. I waited on a wooden bench that was bolted to the floor. At the far end of the corridor was a high mesh-covered window. The tree branches outside moving back and forth in the wind cast shadows along the wall.

Mom came out of her bedroom. The last time I'd seen her, when I'd tried to get her to go to a shrink, her hair had been a beautiful white—almost phosphorescent. Now, just a couple of weeks later, it had gone the yellow of old piano keys. Her face was gray. As she shuffled down the hall, her bathrobe flapped open. Her nightgown was stained at the crotch. When I hugged her, she pressed against me—her breasts, her thighs . . . A whiff of feces came from her. She stepped back and put her hands to my cheeks and repeated—about my father's ashes—"I was trying to save his gold."

IV

Q. Tell me about the lynching.

A. Why?

Q. It's something you never told me.

A. There's a lot I never told you. You wouldn't let me.

Q. I encouraged you to say anything.

A. Right. Any four-letter word. The rest, what I was thinking, feeling, you didn't care.

Q. I cared.

A. It's too late to prove that, isn't it.

Q. You made being a father a test.

A. You were the teacher. I was the student, remember. I learned what you taught. Anyway, now I have a kid . . . Being a father is a test.

Q. Did I pass?

A. Tell me something *you've* kept secret.

Q. I can't tell you something you don't already know.

A. So you're just my imagination. Not a real ghost.

Q. Oh, I'm real enough.

A. Then, tell me something I've forgotten.

Q. October 5, 1957. Saturday afternoon. We were coming back from Johnson's second-hand bookstore. You'd found *Tarzan and the Ant Men*.

A. I didn't think you ever noticed what I bought.

Q. I found an edition of *Anthony and Cleopatra*.

A. Your favorite play.

Q. In the Rolfe edition I was collecting.

A. Bea has them now.

Q. I wanted her to have them.

A. What did you want me to have?

Q. A wife you didn't have to lie to . . . I stopped at Magnolia Terrace. A three-story house on a narrow plot. No front lawn. A dormer window on the third floor. Do you remember? I told you to wait. I went inside. After twenty minutes, you got restless and came into the house. I heard you close the front door and walk from room to empty room on the first floor, climb the stairs, pausing at the landing as if you were thinking about going back down. Do you remember? I heard your steps coming along the hall. The door was open. Do you remember? The bedroom door. I looked back over my shoulder—do you remember—and saw you standing in the doorway, watching me fuck—

A. Janice Tripp.

Q. You remember.

A. Your back was hairy and looked humped. You were on hands and knees. Over her.

Q. Satisfied?

A. You looked like a dog with a scrap of meat. Snarling at another dog to warn it off.

Q. You have such contempt for me.

A. I don't know what I feel about remembering that.

Q. You knew I saw you standing in the doorway.

A. You never said anything.

Q. Neither did you.

A. I was twelve years old. What did you expect me to say?

Q. Ten, fifteen minutes later, I came downstairs. You were waiting for me in the car.

A. I thought you were going to hit me.

Q. I thought you were going to tell your mother.

A. I wanted to protect you.

Q. You wanted to kill me.

A. That, too.

Q. On the way home, I erased the prices in the books we'd bought at Johnson's.

A. The way you always did.

Q. Your mother resented every dime I spent on books and records.

A. And you said—I remember this very well—*Sometimes it's important to shade the truth a little* . . . You made me feel the same way the librarian made me feel when I saw the lynching.

Q. Do you still wish I were alive?

A. At my twenty-fifth high school reunion, I learned a lot about what you were doing back then.

Q. It embarrasses you?

A. It makes it hard to present you sympathetically.

Q. I'd think it would make it harder to present yourself sympathetically. *Say nothing bad of the dead.* Especially if the dead is your father.

A. What about the truth?

Q. Truth? Half of what you remember—you admitted—is filling in the blanks.

A. Your screwing around isn't part of what I'm filling in. At the reunion, Judy Landsman listed half the girls in our class. You'd knock them up, and her father gave them abortions.

Q. I only knocked up one girl.

A. Who?

Q. Your mother knew.

A. I figured. You once told me—I was about to go off to college—*Your mother is a remarkable woman.* Even then I knew what you meant was she was remarkably acquiescent.

My mother sat across from me in the day room, occasionally glancing at me guiltily. Ducking her head and raising her eyebrows. When I reached for her hand, she flinched—and then allowed me to take it in mine.

When I'd gone through her apartment I'd found a single wool mitten on the floor of her closet. I picked it up and carried it around, searching for its mate—which it somehow seemed desperately important to find.

That's what holding my mother's hand felt like.

"Don't be angry!" she screamed. *"Don't be angry!"*

She'd turned her hand over in mine and was clawing at my fingers, as she screamed. *Don't be, don't, don't be angry?* Clawing at my wedding ring. *Don't be, don't be angry* . . . I grabbed her hand in both of mine. Her fingers still moved like insect legs. I squeezed her hand between mine, trying to stop her fingers. Trying to crush them. She looked into my face, oblivious to what her hand was doing. And asked, "Why didn't your father come?"

V

"When I was a little girl," my mother said, "Grandpa used to drive us here on Sundays to look at the grounds."

She leaned on my arm as we walked along a path between two of the red-brick buildings at the state hospital. Other patients sat on benches in bathrobes and slippers, gazing blankly at the perfect lawns. Nurses stood in groups, ignoring the patients and chatting.

"He said that they were as beautiful as the grounds on the Count's estate in Plissa where he grew up," she said.

We sat on one of the benches. It was four o'clock. The sun was low. And the air was getting cold.

"I'm going to spend the rest of my life here, aren't I?" she said.

I started to make some evasive answer, when she interrupted, "Don't bullshit me!"

The nurses were helping the other patients stand and walk back toward the red-brick building.

"Do you know why you're here?" I asked.

"I like the grounds," she said. "They're as beautiful as the estate where Grandpa grew up."

I helped my mother up, held her arm in mine, as she shuffled back toward her ward.

In the middle of the path, she stopped.

"Your father was selfish," she said.

I thought she was going to tell me about all the affairs he'd had.

"You want me to tell you how selfish he was?" she asked.

"No," I said.

"On Sundays, when he'd go to the store to get a loaf of fresh rye, he'd eat both heels. He knew I loved the heels, especially from a loaf of rye. And he'd eat both."

I was trying to save his gold.

A. When she sifted your ashes, she was saving what was best of you.

Q. What was best of me was my spirit. My appetites. I loved being alive!

A. Yes. Your gold. People live metaphors. It wasn't your fillings she was trying to save. Sifting your ashes wasn't revenge.

Q. What was it?

A. Forgiveness.

three ⁓

I

Years ago, when I described my grandfather's death in a novel, my father told me I'd gotten the story backwards.

My father's father—Moisha Ba'er Polishook, called Moses by his American relatives, Mike by everyone else— was a bootlegger, who actually made his bathtub gin in his bathtub, which was in the kitchen of his Lower East Side apartment. A photograph taken in the early 1930s when Mike was forty-six years old shows him naked in the tub, a bowler tilted back on his head. He's smoking a cigar and reading *The Jewish Daily Forward*. He claimed people bought *his* hooch because his body fluids gave it a distinctive flavor.

One day, according to the family story I remember, while my grandfather was bathing in the booze, which was made with something closer to Sterno than ethyl alcohol, a man he'd crossed lit a cigarette and flipped the match into the tub, which exploded into flames.

"Your grandfather wasn't the one who died in a tub," my father said. "He's the one who tossed the match."

And it happened not in the 1930s, my father claimed, but much earlier, possibly before the First World War, although the gin in the tub suggests my father was wrong and it happened during Prohibition.

As the man burned, my grandfather poured himself a shot of *schnapps*, drank it, and, tipping his hat to the horrified wife, sauntered out.

According to my father, the man my grandfather murdered had raped the fifteen-year-old sister of one of my grandfather's gang, a *shaigetz*, an assimilated *Sephardic* Jew, who had left his wealthy family to hang out with low companions like my grandfather.

My great-aunt Florence, called Fifee, who moved to Philadelphia in 1928 to work as a seamstress in Keith's vaudeville theater, told me the raped girl was a Cardozo, New York Jewish aristocracy, who had come to the Lower East Side to patch things up between her brother and her father.

And there is a *New York Times* article about a Rebecca Cardozo who died on April 7, 1919, after being assaulted outside the kosher restaurant at 92 Second Avenue, owned by Abe "the Rabbi" Rabbelle, which was a meeting place for pimps.

But, by 1919, my grandfather had already disappeared.

According to Bernard Schulman's *Shtarkes, Shnorrers, and Shlemiels: Marginal Jewish Life at the Turn of the Century*, "Moses Polishook, who ran a protection racket from 1906 to 1915, murdered one of Abie Dogshitz's Nickel-and-Dime Boys in a bizarre duel over a girl who had been raped in a back room at a Houston Street dance hall."

Abie's last name came from a town near Minsk. But, because of its homophone in America, he was known on the Lower East Side as *Dogshits Abe*. He was a pimp who preyed on girls just arrived in New York. Dogshits worked the West 30s, but around 1910 he was branching out into the Lower East Side. The hoodlum my grandfather murdered was one of the pioneers Dogshits sent into the Neighborhood: Frank *Kishkas* Galembas.

My grandfather waited for *Kishkas* on Allen Street under the Third Avenue El, the heart of the ghetto whorehouse district, the first place in America where brothels identified themselves with red lights. When *Kishkas* stumbled, drunk, out of a tenement, my grandfather splashed him with kerosene. Then, my grandfather emptied a second pail of kerosene over his own head.

Nathan Lippenholtz, my grandfather's cousin, handed both *Kishkas* and my grandfather matches.

"Light them and throw them," my grandfather said.

"You light a match, you catch fire," *Kishkas* protested.

Holding his arms away from his body, my grandfather lit a match and tossed it at *Kishkas*, who danced backward. My grandfather lit and threw another match, which also missed. Advancing on *Kishkas*, disregarding his own danger, my grandfather kept lighting and throwing matches, until *Kishkas*, to defend himself, started doing the same. In the dark, the two men looked like they were throwing stars at each other. My grandfather finally backed *Kishkas* against a wall. He stepped close, struck a match, and snapped it at *Kishkas'* face, which lit up with a halo. As *Kishkas* burned, my grandfather calmly stripped off his own kerosene-soaked clothes, put on a red velvet dressing gown and a fez, and, smoking a cigar, walked into the night, whistling his favorite song, an old vaudeville tune from *A Trip to Chinatown*, "Reuben and Cynthia."

In this version of the story, the raped girl was from the Neighborhood. The girl's name was not recorded.

I'm not sure which story is apocryphal—or as my grandmother would have said, a *bobeh myseh*, an old wives' tale—maybe both are; but, like Biblical legend, the Flood or Joshua tumbling the walls of Jericho with trumpets, there is probably a seed of truth to the tale.

Maybe both versions happened.

My grandfather was struggling to consolidate his control over the Neighborhood, Little Warsaw, and he was known for flamboyant gestures, which scared off competition.

During the first decade of the century, Dogshits Abe was one of only two gangsters who challenged my grandfather's power.

The other gangster was Jack Zelig.

In *Prostitution & Prejudice: The Jewish Fight against White Slavery 1870–1939*, Edward J. Bristow calls Zelig the Robin Hood of the Lower East Side.

When the Italians began recruiting Jewish girls for prostitution, Zelig swore to drive them out of the Neighborhood— not because he objected to prostitution, but because he objected to Italians.

The Italians beat him up, so Zelig, Whitey Lewis, Lefty Louie, Benny Weiss, the pickpocket, and some others confronted the leader of the Italian gang, Jules "The Wop" Morello, at the Avenue Boys' Ball, which was held at the Stuyvesant Casino. As Morello's gang ran, Zelig shot Morello four times. After that, the Italians stayed out of the Neighborhood.

Zelig hung out at Rabbelle's cafe with Whitey, Lefty, Benny the pickpocket, "King Solomon" Kastner, "Shammes" Frank, "Kid Rags," Red Phillips, "Nigger Rue," "Sam Boston," "Crazy Itch," and "The Mohel," who got his name from his habit of castrating his enemies.

In those days, gangsters were divided into those like my grandfather who had nothing to do with prostitution, those like Zelig who ran prostitutes—*nafkis*—with their other businesses, which usually included loan sharking, strike-breaking, drug dealing, and robbery, and the *macks* or pimps like Dogshits who specialized in prostitution.

My grandfather tolerated Zelig even though Zelig tolerated prostitution. And Zelig respected my grandfather— or feared him—enough to leave him alone.

In late 1910 or early 1911, my grandfather sent Zelig an emissary, a hood named only "Poopik," which means Bellybutton. A photograph taken of Poopik ten years later on a slab in the morgue shows a man with hooded, almost oriental eyes and a chin cleft like a baby's bottom. He appears to be in his mid-twenties, which means, when he played ambassador to Zelig, he had probably just celebrated his Bar Mitzvah. Poopik told Zelig my grandfather wanted to arrange a formal truce.

Zelig and my grandfather met at dawn at the Washington Poultry Market. A New York Historical Society photograph of the market at 6 A.M. in the early part of the century shows the morning sun slanting through the stacked cages and throwing shadows of bars onto what looks like a plank sidewalk. The stench and the noise from the birds must have been overwhelming.

My grandfather offered to get rid of Dogshits, who was Zelig's chief rival in the prostitution business.

Dogshits was attacking Zelig's pimps, spreading word that Zelig's whores were syphilitic, and threatening or bribing Zelig's watchboys to steer prospects to his own whorehouses. Dogshits even got little kids to steal the washed strips of cloth, used for sanitary napkins, which Zelig's girls hung outside their windows to dry. And, the final insult, Dogshits invited Zelig's most expensive whore, Anna "The Golden Fleece" Dubinsky, to Steckles', the Third Avenue Restaurant where the high-rollers dined.

When Zelig asked my grandfather why he wanted to do this favor, my grandfather, evasive, told the following story:

In Warsaw, just before the turn of the century, a traveling circus advertised a battle to the death between a lion and a tiger. Both animals—the circus promised—were untamed and both had been starved to make them even more savage.

But the day of the performance, the tiger died. Not knowing what to do, the owner of the circus hid in a bar to get drunk. A Jew overheard his plight and offered to disguise himself in the tiger's skin and fight the lion.

"Why would you do such a crazy thing?" the circus owner asked.

"I can't get work," the Jew said, "and, without a job,

I'm sure to die anyway. At least, this way I have a chance. If I kill the lion, you pay me a hundred pieces of gold."

The circus owner agreed and arranged to have the tiger skinned.

That night, the Jew, dressed in the tiger skin, prowled into the circus tent. The stink of the freshly gutted animal filled his nostrils. The shouts of the crowd filled his ears. At the other end of the arena waited the lion, who roared and crouched, ready to attack.

The Jew lost heart and, convinced he was about to die, recited his death prayer, "*Shema Yisroel!* Hear O Israel—"

"*Adonoy Elohenu Adonoy Echod!*" said the lion, finishing the prayer.

Amazed, the Jew looked closer and realized that the lion was also a man disguised in an animal skin.

"What are you doing here?" the Jew asked.

"What?" the lion said. "You think you're the only Jew who needs a job?"

I suspect my grandfather's decision to join forces with Zelig against Dogshits had something to do with his duel with *Kishkas*.

Zelig wanted to know how my grandfather intended to handle Dogshits and what he wanted if he succeeded.

"How," my grandfather said, "is my secret. What I want . . . well, time will tell."

A week after the Poultry Market summit conference, my grandfather, dressed in his best suit, his hair lacquered with Brilliantine, appeared with Tateh Kroll, the Neighborhood holy man, at the whorehouse Dogshits had opened on Allen Street.

When I was a boy, my father used to tell me bedtime

stories about Tateh Kroll—like the time Tateh Kroll stopped God from destroying the Earth by distracting Him with a shaggy-dog story while the last person needed to make up the Saving Remnant was born.

Or the time Tateh Kroll was nursing the most beautiful woman in the Neighborhood, when the Angel of Death appeared. As Death took the woman in his arms, there was a knock at the door.

"Her husband!" Tateh Kroll told Death. "He's insanely jealous. If he finds you here with his wife, no telling what he'll do."

So Death, which everyone knows is a coward, changed clothes with Tateh Kroll, who had just taken Death's scythe when the door opened to reveal an old woman Tateh Kroll had sent to Rubin's Restaurant for some chicken soup.

Relieved, Death asked Tateh Kroll for his cloak and scythe—"quick, before her husband comes."

"She doesn't have a husband," Tateh Kroll admitted. In order to get his cloak and scythe back, Death had to promise to leave without the woman, who recovered and married a dentist on the Upper West Side.

One Passover, Elijah, the Prophet, who visits every Seder in the world, arrived at Tateh Kroll's table, looking poorly.

"What's the matter?" Tateh Kroll asked.

"The Lord said, *Be fruitful and multiply*," Elijah sighed, "and who am I to gainsay the Lord. But do you know how many Seders I've been to tonight? I have one more visit to make, and I am exhausted."

"Rest here," Tateh Kroll said. "I'll go in your stead."

"Are you sure you can handle the job?" Elijah asked.

"What's to handle," Tateh Kroll said. "I go in, drink the wine, and come home."

So, while Elijah rested at Tateh Kroll's table, Tateh Kroll went to the last Seder.

Around midnight, Tateh Kroll returned.

"So?" Elijah asked.

"Not to worry," Tateh Kroll said. "I had a wonderful time."

All year Elijah was troubled. Never before had he missed a household. What if Tateh Kroll had done something wrong?

The following Passover, Elijah hurried through his rounds, anxious to get to the last Seder where Tateh Kroll had taken his place. Finally, he arrived.

The door had been left open as it should have been. Elijah peeked in. The table was properly set; the *Haggadahs* opened to the proper page. Everything looked okay.

Elijah breathed a sigh of relief—and entered.

The family turned with delight. But, when they saw Elijah, their faces fell and they asked, "What happened to the guy who was here last year?"

Everyone in the Neighborhood loved Tateh Kroll and held him in awe. No one, not even the most brutal thug, would bother him.

My grandfather sat Tateh Kroll down in the whorehouse parlor, where Tateh Kroll started to read aloud from the *Pentateuch*—*Genesis:* "In the beginning God created the heaven and the earth . . ."

For five nights, Tateh Kroll read the *Scripture* in the

whorehouse while my grandfather greeted the men who came, giving them tea and spongecake.

In the presence of the holy man, the men were too ashamed to spend money on the whores, who in any case sat in their silk and satin wrappers on the floor around Tateh Kroll, listening. Even Dogshits' hoods, intimidated by Tateh Kroll, stood by idly.

On the sixth night, Dogshits surrendered and agreed to leave the Lower East Side.

On the seventh day, my grandfather rested.

In 1912, when Red Phillips murdered Zelig, there was no one left to challenge my grandfather's control.

In the Neighborhood, where there had been warring gangs, there was now one gang. And no more war.

II

When I was a kid, I overheard someone describe my grandfather as the Pasha of Allen Street. I had a book—a child's version of *The Arabian Nights*, I think—which had an illustration of a pasha: a fat man in ballooning red pantaloons, a comically small red vest covering a pink hairless chest, and a turban with an ostrich feather that towered over his head.

Nothing like my grandfather.

But from 1912 to 1919, in the Neighborhood, my grandfather ruled like an oriental potentate.

In a report on Jewish criminality at the turn of the century written by Abe Shoenfeld, a Jewish detective working for the Kehillah, my grandfather was described as "a low gangster, addicted to vice, who affected a boule-vardier's elegance, as he made his evening rounds."

The photograph in the book, attributed to a student of Jacob Riis, shows a dapper man of medium build with a trim mustache, a bowler tilted back on his head, a boiled white shirt, and a stiff high collar. He leans against the wall of a synagogue, Temple Emanu-El—which is odd, since he rarely went to any *schul*, never to that one.

I suspect his pose—and its location—was his way of giving respectable society the finger. Temple Emanu-El's rabbi, Gustav Gottheil, founded the Society to Aid Jewish Prisoners, which was established to help the fifty-five Jewish convicts at Sing-Sing and Auburn and to prevent Jewish crime.

Rabbi Gottheil—like many Jews and non-Jews—believed Russian and Polish Jews, like my grandfather, had overly-developed criminal instincts.

But my grandfather was as much rabbi as gangster.

From three in the afternoon until midnight, he sat at his table in the back of Nisanoff's, a cafe on Houston Street, noshing on pickled tomatoes, drinking Turkish coffee, and resolving quarrels among neighbors.

A picture, taken by the same woman who photographed my grandfather at Temple Emanu-El, Edith Morgan, shows my grandfather holding court. His back is reflected in a mirror. His hair is so smooth and glossy it looks like the painted head of a ceramic doll—except for the base of his skull, where the pomade was ineffective and his hair made a quarter-sized nebula-shaped whorl. His left ear sticks out from his head and has an odd crimp in the top like a dog-eared page. His celluloid collar, the drape of the coat, the creases in his sleeves gathering into a *V* where each elbow presses the sides of his chair . . . Everything is stretched, everything is tight. From the back, he looks tense.

From the front, however, he looks relaxed. His face has an abstracted, almost indolent expression: half-closed eyes, half-smiling mouth. His head is tilted to one side, listening . . . Even the cloth of his coat is more relaxed, falling in loose folds.

Two men. One tense, one relaxed. Which one was my grandfather? From eighty years later, I seem to be looking at him from behind the mirror, from the back—or, at least, from backstage. The tension reflected in the mirror, the part of him that did not face the world, the part he was unaware of, strikes me as the more accurate.

The troubles people wanted him to solve were, for the most part, domestic. A cousin newly-arrived from the Old World who felt she was being treated like a maid by the American relatives who took her in, a loan that was not repaid, a chamber pot accidentally emptied out a window onto someone else's drying laundry . . . According to most accounts, my grandfather, an Allen Street Solomon, could calm the feuding neighbors, because he was fair.

One story that survives from that time tells of two women who complained to my grandfather that a man— Yitsak Barber or Berber, reports differ about his last name—had made a marriage contract with them both. Even though Berber—or Barber—was clearly a scoundrel, neither woman wanted to give him up. Each insisted he honor his commitment. My grandfather couldn't understand why they so irrationally loved the man, but pleased them both without pleasing Barber—or Berber—who wanted to marry neither. My grandfather decreed that from January to June Berber—or Barber—would live with one woman and from July to December he would live with the other. All year, he would support them both.

Legal? No. Fair? Maybe. In any case, Barber—or Berber—agreed. My grandfather had the power to enforce his judgments.

My grandfather's reputation for wisdom and fairness was so great that, once, God sent an Angel to the Neighborhood to ask my grandfather's advice on what to do about mankind, which, no matter what God did, still strayed from the paths of righteousness.

The Angel appeared in the form of a tramp with a filthy coat, the green of pond scum, and a wall eye, which, when he looked straight at you, seemed to be angled off to the side. It also meant that, when he didn't appear to be looking at you, the Angel could be scrutinizing your every move. The toe of his left shoe flapped open like the mouth of a puppet.

Used to dealing with the boss of other gangs, my grandfather was insulted that God had sent an underling.

"If God wants to talk to me," my grandfather told the Angel, "let him come Himself."

The Angel departed.

The next night, the Angel returned in a blaze of glory. Its wings, vibrating faster than a hummingbird's, made a sound like a hurricane. Its face burned like the mouth of a furnace, radiating an unbearable heat. Over its countenance flickered dark spots like blemishes, which were even hotter than the rest of its features. Its eyes were as hungry as the eyes of a wolf in winter, waiting at the edge of a village, slavering, wanting yet afraid to attack a stray chicken or, even better, a child on the way to the outhouse.

My grandfather repeated what he'd told the Angel the previous night: "If God wants to talk to me, let him come Himself."

"You don't know what you're asking," the Angel said. "God is terrible. When Abraham spoke God's word in Nimrod's palace, he shook the throne and all the idols Nimrod worshipped fell on their faces in fear and awe. For two hours, Nimrod lay trembling. At last, he dared raise his eyes to Abraham and ask, *Is that the voice of God?* Abraham said, *No. That was merely the voice of the least of his creatures.*"

"Nevertheless," my grandfather said, "I will talk only to Him."

The next night, God Himself, the Lord of Hosts, blessed be He, was waiting when my grandfather arrived at his usual time at Nisanoff's. God sat at the back of the restaurant at my grandfather's table. My grandfather noticed that God sat in my grandfather's chair. But my grandfather decided not to make an issue of it.

My grandfather sent everyone out of the cafe and locked the door. People pressed their faces against the window, watching as my grandfather poured Slivovitz for them both.

They raised their glasses, toasted each other, and drank down the brandy, which—God conceded—was the best He'd ever had.

"It's local," my grandfather said. "You should stop by more often."

They gossiped about the Neighborhood, about how Mordke Blum, the tailor, had tried to gyp Jerry Reckless over a bolt of gabardine, about how the Gelphy brothers watered their beer, about how Ticklish Gittel beat up her pimp because he wouldn't buy her a new hat. My grandfather, who always suspected that Haimovitch cheated at cards, tried to get God to tell him if he was right.

But God said, "Moisha, Moisha, what would you have Me—the Lord of Hosts—be? A stool-pigeon?"

My grandfather shrugged and said, "*You* don't have to play cards with Haimovitch."

My grandfather refilled their glasses, wondering if God ever got drunk. And what would happen if He did . . .

After they had finished their second glass of Slivovitz and my grandfather had poured a third, my grandfather said, "So, you want to know what to do with mankind?"

His tone was the same one he used when young toughs came to him with schemes and my grandfather put them off by saying, "If you're so smart, why aren't you rich?"

Nothing God did kept mankind from sin.

"I've tried flood," God said, "I've leveled whole cities, nothing seems to do the trick."

God told my grandfather the *real* story of Adam and Eve, which we know is true because it appears in the Pseudepigrapha, the *Life of Adam and Eve*.

Everyone knows that Adam and Eve sinned by eating the fruit of the forbidden Tree of the Knowledge of Good and Evil, which God confided was not an apple tree but a date palm. But few people know that God tried to give them a second chance.

God said Adam could expiate his guilt by standing

neck-deep in the Tigris River with a rock on his head for sixty days. Eve had to stand neck-deep in the Euphrates with a rock on her head for fifty-nine days.

Adam and Eve did what they were told.

While Eve stood in the Euphrates—neck-deep with a rock on her head, as she was supposed to—the Serpent came to the river bank and asked her what she was doing.

When she explained, the Serpent asked how standing neck-deep in water with a stone for a hat could expiate her guilt?

"You know," Eve said to the Serpent, "you're right. It doesn't make sense."

So Eve took the stone off her head, climbed out of the water, and walked to where Adam stood in the Tigris.

"Adam," Eve said, "I was just talking to the Serpent and . . ."

Adam slapped his forehead in despair.

"Not again!" he said.

"You see, Moisha," God explained to my grandfather, "no matter how many chances I give people, they still screw up."

"Like my kids," my grandfather said, "but what can you do?"

God sighed.

"I guess, no matter what, you just have to love them," my grandfather said.

"Well . . . ," God said, standing. He left the sentence unfinished.

"Anytime you're in the Neighborhood . . . ," my grandfather said, also standing.

"I'm always in the Neighborhood," God said. "And everywhere else. You know that."

"Sometimes," my grandfather said, "it doesn't seem like it."

III

During his reign, my grandfather appeared, by all accounts, content. He loved his wife, Sarah, and his children—especially his children, my father, who was so rowdy, and his older brother, Max, who was so stupid that my grandfather called them *Tohu* and *Bohu*, *Chaos* and *Emptiness*.

When I was going off to college—a WASP school in New England, with a white-painted church in the center of a campus on a hill overlooking the orange, red, and yellow autumn landscape, a world very different from Allen Street and Nisanoff's in the dawn of the century—my father embarrassed me in front of my new dorm by hugging me and kissing me good-by. Seeing my discomfort, my father tried to explain: "Now I know what *my* father meant when he said the love a man has for his children is greater than any love he could have for a woman."

It's taken me thirty years—and fathering two children myself—to understand what my father and *his* father meant.

In 1918, when my father was nine years old, Dogshits Abe returned to the Neighborhood in the company of two gentiles: an older man and a young woman.

The woman was Edith Morgan, the photographer who a few months later would take the pictures of my grandfather in front of Temple Emanu-El and inside Nisanoff's. The man was her husband, Raymond.

Raymond Morgan—who was twice Edith's age—was a very ill, very rich man, who burned with two missions: to raise poor immigrant Jews from their squalor and to convert them to Christianity. His entry in *The Dictionary of National Biography* describes him as a lawyer and sportsman, both of which he had been as a younger man. He was an indifferent polo player, a mediocre hunter with a camp in the Adirondacks, a member of the Jockey, Racquet, and Union League clubs, and a group which called themselves the *Seven*.

The original *Seven* was formed by James Gordon Bennett, Jr. during his exile in France. He had to leave New York after one drunken New Year's, when he either pissed or threw up in his fiancée's—later his ex-fiancée's—fireplace. In Paris, he became the pivot around which young American expatriates whirled. At a late dinner, one of Bennett's visitors—a Harvard student named Chandler—bragged that he could seduce a Mme. Noilles, who was notorious for being faithful to her husband. Bennett scoffed. Chandler, both profligate and confident, said he would bet them $10,000 he would succeed. There were seven at dinner, Bennett, Chandler, and five others: the *Seven*, who gave the club its name. Four additional friends joined the six who bet Chandler, each putting up $1,000. Ten to one odds. Chandler was *very* profligate. *Very* confident.

He would prove he had won the bet by getting Mme. Noilles to give him some intimate token of affection—which turned out to be a cameo.

Bennett and the other expatriates each paid the Harvard student the thousand dollars they had bet. And they formalized the club, which, although still called the *Seven*, continued to grow.

Each year, the *Seven* offered membership to someone selected from their circle who put up $10,000 and was challenged to seduce a married woman with a reputation for faithfulness. If the prospective member failed to make love to the woman and return with an intimate token, he lost his money, which went into the club's treasury—and he was rejected for membership. If the prospective member succeeded, he was formally inducted during the club's annual dinner and the token he brought back was mounted on the clubhouse wall along with all the other souvenirs, which by the 1960s included everything from G-strings to diaphragms. The club was disbanded, because, according to one of its last members, there were no longer any faithful wives to seduce.

Raymond was the third member to be inducted after the original band. And he was the only member in the club's eighty-year history to fall in love with the woman he seduced and marry her.

He was a nephew of Bessie Hamilton Morgan, the first wife of August Belmont, Jr.—a serendipitous connection, since a dozen years before I learned about his association with my family I wrote a biography of August Belmont, Sr.

Except for his membership in the *Seven*, until his mid-fifties, Raymond seems to have lived an unremarkable life. Even within his family, he remained a figure dim enough to present only a ghostly impression, flickering at the edges of their consciousness, usually mentioned, when mentioned at all, as the last in a list of people present at some event— as in, "We had a wonderful time in Lenox with Augie,

Perry, little Mary, Eleanor, Corinne, Frederick, Lowell, Seth, and Raymond."

When he was fifty-two years old, Raymond lost his first wife, the woman he had seduced two decades earlier. He mourned for five years, month by month growing dimmer, so dim finally he seems to have been in danger of disappearing altogether. In a letter written in 1913, one of his cousins remarked that Raymond had become so spectral that he "no longer lived in his house, he haunted it."

To pull him out of his gloom, some friends took him on a sail up the Nile—by houseboat, a *dahabeah*—and a tour of the Holy Land.

During the trip, his life was changed by two significant events. He met Edith Clews, soon to be his second wife— my grandfather's photographer. And he underwent a conversion of some sort, something vivifying enough to bring him into clear focus for his family and friends.

In a letter from my Belmont files, August, Jr. describes Raymond, after he had returned from the trip, as being "in love and in the grip of a new enthusiasm for the exotic. I don't know which is worse."

He began his dual mission to save the Jews.

After Raymond married Edith, he'd bring her to the Lower East Side. She didn't share his passion for either philanthropy or evangelism, but she was as fascinated as he was by the Neighborhood's exoticism. She discovered the work of Jacob Riis. And, influenced by him, translated an amusement with amateur photography into a passion equal to her husband's but one for recording a world which she correctly suspected would soon be gone.

Their guide to this world was Dogshits.

I have no idea how Raymond and Edith came to hire him. Maybe someone from Raymond's circle met Dogshits on a visit to one of his uptown brothels, one of the dollar houses in the Tenderloin. Maybe Dogshits supplied artist's models for New York's bohemia, where some of Edith's acquaintances slummed.

However he met them, Dogshits used them to invade my grandfather's territory. With them, he'd be safe. When my grandfather drove Dogshits out of the Lower East Side, he may have done him a favor, because, when Dogshits reappeared, he was transformed: his clothes, his manners, his speech had all become American. He was no longer Abe Dogshits. He was Abraham Diamond.

And my grandfather was not the Pasha of Allen Street. He was a specimen Jew.

IV

Edith thought my grandfather had an interesting face. My grandfather thought Edith was the most beautiful woman he had ever seen. She asked if she could take a series of portraits. He agreed in order to be in her company. Edith's husband Raymond wanted to save my grandfather. Edith was the agent of his destruction.

According to family legend, as my grandfather asked Edith and her husband about where they lived, about *how* they lived, a woman arrived with an infant, who she claimed had been born with a *dybbuk*. By not feeding the baby, she hoped to starve the demon out. But the *dybbuk* was stubborn and refused to leave the body of her son, who had become ill from lack of nourishment.

My grandfather questioned the woman, who said she had arrived from Lithuania three months before the baby was born. Then, my grandfather questioned the *dybbuk*, who, speaking in Yiddish from the baby's belly, said that he'd possessed the baby while it was still in the woman's womb.

"So," my grandfather said, "you come from the Old World. You're a Litvak *dybbuk*."

"Better than being a *Galitzianer*," the *dybbuk* said.

"Why did you enter this woman's baby?" my grandfather asked.

"Like everyone else," the *dybbuk* said, "I wanted to come to the *goldeneh medina*, the Golden Land."

"The Golden Land!" my grandfather said, gesturing at the filthy street, which could be seen through the cafe window. "Does *that* look like a Golden Land to you? *These people*—" my grandfather pointed at Edith and Raymond— "*they* live in a Golden Land!"

And he told the *dybbuk* what Edith and Raymond had been telling *him* of their life—*his* version of what they had been telling him: They lived in a mansion with a hundred rooms. Each room had a hundred doors. Each door concealed a hundred servants, who were waiting to cater to a hundred desires. Their ceilings were so high they were hidden by clouds. Their beds were as big as ships. Their pillows were as soft as a whore's belly. They ate off plates of gold the color of blood oranges. Their chandeliers glistened like moonlight on snow.

"Why stay in the Neighborhood," my grandfather said, "when you can go uptown and live in a palace?"

My grandfather knew *dybbuks* like luxury.

"How will I get uptown?" the *dybbuk* asked.

"I'll give you a nickel for the subway," my grandfather said—and put the coin on the table.

The *dybbuk* climbed out of the baby's mouth. It was an inch tall and looked like a pig with a human face, the face of a wizened old man. It crossed the table, its cloven hooves tapping like a tinker's hammer. When it went to pick up the nickel, my grandfather clapped a glass over it, capturing it.

As everyone crowded around to examine the strange creature, the *dybbuk*—inside the glass—cursed my grandfather and took the Lord's name in vain. Finally, it gave up and sat on its haunches, glowering at my grandfather.

Raymond—according to family legend—took the *dybbuk* home with him as a curiosity and kept it in an aquarium in his study, feeding it oysters, lobster, and other *traif* food, in exchange for which it entertained the *goyim* by telling anti-Semitic jokes and singing obscene songs like its version of the *Had-gad-yoh*, in which, at the end, God does not slay the Angel of Death, but conceives upon it a generation of monsters.

For the next few months, two or three times a week, Edith came to Nisanoff's to talk to my grandfather and take his photograph.

My grandmother—Sarah—was suspicious of Edith. But not jealous. She was too proud to be jealous. And too beautiful, as beautiful as the Biblical Sarah.

My grandmother had a dark olive complexion, almond-shaped eyes, high cheekbones, full lips, and a voluptuous figure. You could imagine her emerging from a goat-skin tent in the wilderness, walking through a field of wild barley, or drawing water from a well like Rebekah or Rachel. Or playing upon the timbrel and dancing like Miriam. Or seducing and killing an enemy of her people like Judith. She was as pious as Susanna, as brave as Esther, as charismatic as Deborah . . . My grandfather's cousin, Nathan Lippenholtz, used to say that my grandmother could have been the Shulamite in *The Song of Songs: Thine eyes are as doves behind thy veil . . . Thy lips are like a thread of scarlet . . . Thy two breasts are like two fawns . . . which feed among the lilies . . . Thy navel is like a round goblet wherein no mingled wine is wanting . . . Thy belly is like a heap of wheat set about with lilies . . . The smell of thy countenance like apples . . .* In the Neighborhood, people called my grandmother the Rose of Sharon.

My grandmother objected to how much time my grandfather was spending with Edith.

My grandfather said that, as a leader of the Neighborhood, he couldn't deny Edith the opportunity to take his photograph.

My grandmother said it wasn't the photographs she was worried about.

My grandfather said Edith came to him like anyone else—to ask his advice, to hear his stories.

And to drink with you, my grandmother said.

And to drink with me, my grandfather admitted.

My grandmother reminded my grandfather of the story

in the Midrash about the Jew captured by heathens, who said they would spare him if he committed one of three sins: Get drunk, have sexual intercourse with one of their women, or bow down before their idols.

The Jew chose the least of the three sins: To get drunk.

But he got so drunk that he had intercourse with one of their women and bowed down before their idol.

My grandfather said my grandmother didn't understand a woman like Edith.

My grandmother said she understood enough.

My grandfather said discussing Edith with my grandmother . . . *Es iz vert a zets in dred.* It was as futile as stomping on the earth!

My father and my uncle were delighted by Edith. She smelled of spring flowers. And brought them presents. Tops that spun like rainbows. Tin dogs that swallowed pennies, pennies she gave them. Soldiers—*soldiers!* my grandmother exclaimed, *in Russian uniforms, Austrian uniforms, uniforms of countries that persecuted the Jews.*

My grandmother threw out the toys and said, "No more presents!"

My grandfather took Edith around the Neighborhood. Everywhere they went, people crowded around them, eager to see the *shiksa* goddess, who took their pictures and later brought back the photographs, which troubled them.

People in the Neighborhood were used to having their pictures taken in studios, in front of velvet curtains, with a Grecian column to one side, everyone dressed in their best clothes and arranged around a throne where the Papa sat.

Instead, in Edith's photographs, they saw themselves dressed in work clothes, sweaty, going about their daily business.

In Edith's photographs, they recognized themselves as they were. In the studio photographs, they recognized themselves as they wished to be.

Kallikak, the Neighborhood photographer, spread a rumor that Edith's pictures were sly insults.

"Uptown, among the Goyim," Kallikak said, "she shows the pictures and says, *See how dirty the Jews are.*"

The shopkeepers, the elders, the pious objected to the photographs, because Edith took pictures of gangsters and whores, of guttersnipes and gigolos. They formed a Committee, which approached my grandmother, who was the only one who could stop what they saw as my grandfather's folly.

Folly? my grandmother said. It was worse than folly.

By letting Edith record the Neighborhood life with all its imperfections, my grandmother claimed my grandfather was betraying the Jews.

Betraying the Jews!

My grandfather's wife was accusing him of the worse sin someone in the Neighborhood could commit—worse than rape or murder, worse even than ignoring the Sabbath . . . The measure by which all other measures were measured was: *Is it good for the Jews?*

The Neighborhood had decided Edith and her photographs were *not* good for the Jews!

When Dogshits heard about my grandfather's trouble, he crowed.

Dogshits had hoped Edith and Raymond would be not

just his safe-conduct in the Neighborhood, but would, unaware, give him a beachhead from which he could regain his power. But my grandfather had usurped his position with Edith and Raymond, once again shutting him out.

Now, Dogshits could get his revenge.

He rushed to the Committee.

Newly respectable, with his banker's suit, and accent-less English, he offered himself as their Savior.

True, Dogshits admitted, in the past he'd been a whore-monger.

But, look at him, he'd become a respectable business-man, a landlord with many tenements.

As for my grandfather, he had even given up holding court every afternoon and evening at Nisanoff's. He had less time to resolve the Neighborhood's quarrels. Two or three times a week, he headed uptown.

What he did there, no one knew—although there were rumors: Stories of how he mingled with Edith's friends, who in their imaginations no matter what the hour or occasion all wore white tie and tails; how he ate off Edith's plates, mingling meat and dairy; how he performed adulterous acts under Edith's husband's roof, sometimes while her husband was there.

According to my father, my grandfather went uptown to Edith's house only once. For an uncomfortable hour, my grandfather sat, chatting with Edith and her friends; then, trying to surprise the goyim with his knowledge of gentile things, he did a *kazatska*, a Cossack dance. What, my grandfather thought, could be *less* Jewish?

The nuance was lost on Edith and her friends, who enjoyed but were puzzled by this dapper man with the funny accent in the—to them—shabby clothes, who, in the middle of tea, squatted in the parlor, crossed his arms over his chest, and, with whoops, started twirling and leaping, his legs shooting out from under him as if he were defying gravity.

When my grandfather left Edith's house, he realized for the first time that beyond the Neighborhood was a great world in which he was an insignificant—even comical—figure.

It was a world he could not enter. He decided never again to see Edith.

That night, when my grandfather arrived at Nisanoff's, the Committee was waiting for him. Watching from the back of the room was Dogshits—in his American topcoat, with one leg casually crossed over the other in the American way, the way Edith's friends had crossed their legs as they watched my grandfather dance. The Committee told my grandfather that they had discussed his recent negligence,

his treachery—and had decided to replace him with his cousin Lippenholtz.

Mutiny!

Dogshits smiled. He could handle Lippenholtz.

My grandfather crossed the room, grabbed Dogshits by the throat, ran him toward the front of the cafe, and threw him through the plateglass window into the street.

Then, he turned to the Committee and said, "What were you saying?"

Everyone shuffled and avoided meeting my grandfather's gaze—except Lippenholtz, who calmly repeated that they had decided they could no longer trust my grandfather.

My grandfather turned to the Committee and asked, "Is that what you think?"

No one answered.

My grandfather turned to Lippenholtz and repeated, "Is that what you think?"

"Yes," Lippenholtz said.

My grandfather sat in his accustomed chair. A waiter poured him a glass of Slivovitz—so nervously that he spilled a little. My grandfather took a sip and said:

"When King David was an old man, his best friend—thinking he was acting in the interests of the people—betrayed him. The man was brought before the King, who with tears in his eyes passed the only sentence he could: Death."

Everyone in the cafe looked at Lippenholtz, who looked at my grandfather.

"But, since the man had been King David's friend," my grandfather continued, "and since he had acted without self-interest, King David let him choose his manner of death. The man chose death by old age."

My grandfather finished his Slivovitz, stood up, and walked past Lippenholtz, past the Committee, out of the cafe.

According to one story, it was that night he was bathing in his gin when someone—perhaps Edith's husband Raymond, perhaps Dogshits, perhaps someone else, my grandfather had many enemies—flipped the match into the tub.

But, according to Shulman's history of Lower East Side low life, my grandfather never returned home. The last anyone saw of him: He paused before crossing Houston Street, lit a cigar, took a puff, and strolled off into the night, whistling "Reuben and Cynthia."

four

I

In 1880, when my mother's mother—Bella Gordon—was six years old, she was picking mushrooms with her older sister—Ruth—in a wood near Plissa when three men on horseback passed. One of them was wearing a tight-fitting tunic, the brown—my grandmother remembered—of the mushrooms they were gathering. The piping and the strap crossing his chest were a lighter brown, the color of the dirt road. There were parallel red stripes—my grandmother thought two—on his epaulets, collar, and yellow cuff flaps. The uniform of a Lithuanian Guards Officer. His high black boots were covered with dust that reminded my grandmother of the sugar powder on the candy her father once brought home from Vilna, probably Turkish delight. His cap was tilted a little to the side, which she thought was comical. His mustache, waxed and very thin, was crimped

up at the ends, almost a ninety-degree angle. He looked—
my grandmother said—kind, not at all severe and military, the look of a man who liked to play with children. My
grandmother remembered thinking of him as *the Handsome
Soldier*.

One of his companions wore a heavy brown greatcoat,
which made him seem to my grandmother like a bear on
horseback. The sun was behind a cloud. The afternoon was
chilly. She didn't remember anything about the third man,
who never got off his horse—but during the following
events rode a little apart and, without looking back, packed
and smoked a pipe. My grandmother *does* remember the
smell of the pipe, which drifted to her on the breeze, a
sweet smell like burning cherry-wood.

The men, clearly gentiles, came from the officer training
school in the nearby town of Polotsk, which was a center of
anti-Jewish sentiment, partly because of its large Jewish
population, which had grown from 2,600 in 1815, to around
12,000 by the late 1880s.

As the soldiers passed, my grandmother and her sister,
Ruth, stopped looking for mushrooms and, standing by the
side of the road, waited, heads bowed, for the men to pass,
a cautious response.

During the past quarter of a century, when my grandmother's parents were coming of age, when my grandmother and her sister had been born, the government had
been more tolerant of Jews. Czar Alexander II had encouraged assimilation. He allowed Jews to become lawyers. He
reformed laws concerning Jews in the army. He established state schools for Jews, including the State Rabbini-
cal Seminaries, which, later, were replaced by Teachers'

Seminaries. And he allowed Jews to settle beyond the Pale—the area in Russia where Jews traditionally had been permitted to live—and buy land in cities and towns that previously had been barred to them.

Although this policy of assimilation was not always liberal—for example, business letters could not be written in Yiddish and Hebrew—Jews fared better than they had before Alexander II, whom my grandmother, echoing her parents, still, in 1964 when she was ninety years old, called *the good czar*.

But no matter how tolerant the government became, my grandmother and Ruth knew that there was always danger of a reaction.

In fact, the year after the soldiers came upon my grandmother and her sister picking mushrooms—in 1881—Alexander II was assassinated and his successor Alexander III turned on the Jews with a vengeance, demanding that they convert, emigrate, or die.

My grandmother and Ruth were right to stand motionless by the roadside, hoping the soldiers would pass—which they didn't. Two of them stopped.

As they approached my grandmother and Ruth, my grandmother raised her head a little to get a better look at the soldiers.

Under her breath Ruth told her to look down—which gave the Handsome Soldier an excuse to speak to her.

"Why do you scold her?" he asked Ruth, who didn't answer him. "She's very strict, isn't she?" he asked my grandmother, who again dared to glance at him. "You're a pretty child," he told my grandmother—who was pleased by the flattery.

Seventy years later, as she told the story, she blushed, as if she were still six years old standing by the side of a road in Lithuania being complimented by the Handsome Soldier—who was probably dead. We never escape our ghosts.

"Leave her alone," Ruth told the Handsome Soldier.

The other soldier—whom my grandmother thought of as the Bear—urged his friend to stop flirting. They had to be on their way.

But the Handsome Soldier turned back to Ruth.

"Why are you so unfriendly?" he asked her.

Ruth didn't answer.

My grandmother doesn't remember what he said next. She *does* remember him coming very close to them, so close she could smell some scent he wore, something like barley water, which mingled with the smell from the Soldier-on-Horseback's tobacco, the smell of the pines, and the musty smell of the fallen needles, the rotting floor of the forest.

And she remembers the Handsome Soldier gently putting the tips of his fingers—was he wearing gloves? had he taken them off?—under Ruth's chin and slowly raising her face. She also remembers a jingling sound, which may have been his saber or his spurs. And she remembers his oath—a word she refused to repeat when she told the story—when Ruth spit into his face.

"Why did Ruth do that?" I asked.

It was the summer of 1963. I was just about to go off for my freshman year at college and had stopped in Providence to visit my grandparents—my mother's parents—on my way to Cape Cod, one of the first times I'd hitchhiked beyond the limits of my hometown.

I'd arrived late at night, tired and hungry, having walked for hours from downtown Providence, where I'd been dropped off by my last ride, to Congress Avenue, where my grandparents lived.

When I rang their bell, I could see, through the living room windows, lights snapping on at the back of the house—my grandparents' bedroom, the kitchen—getting closer and closer to the front door—the dining room, the living room, and finally the hallway. The thick glass panel on the upper half of the front door was mottled glass, almost opaque. On either side of the door were narrow decorative windows of colored glass, light and dark greens, which left an impression of illuminated vines. Arriving unannounced, waking them up . . . I'd never taken such liberties with my grandparents before.

The door opened. My grandfather—in gray pajamas and a maroon bathrobe, wearing brown slippers, the kind with no heel, looked at me as if my arrival was the most natural thing in the world, as if he'd been expecting me.

In the kitchen, my grandmother—small and busy, in a quilted robe, her hair down around her shoulders, the only time I'd ever seen it loose—made me a bowl of corn flakes and a cup of tea. And we started talking . . .

I talked about my restlessness at home, about wanting to go to interesting places and do exciting things. My grandfather told me some old stories—some of which I used in my first novel—about riding through the fields at harvest time when he was still a boy and how some of the older girls who were haying flirted with him.

His father was a *kulak*, a bailiff. He managed the estate of a count, who gambled and lost and borrowed money from my grandfather's father and got drunk with my grandfather's father and questioned him about Jewish customs and argued about politics—a good man, my grandfather said, a sad man . . .

Because of my grandfather's father's special position, my grandfather was brought up like a young prince.

"All the girls loved him," my grandmother said.

Her family—which came from the same town—was not so fortunate. They distrusted my grandfather's father—and warned her against my grandfather, who was seen as a dangerous young man, "a Romeo," my grandmother called him.

In the early morning light coming through the kitchen windows, I—seventeen years old—examined my grandfather, who, with his serenity, his white hair, and his love, I had as a child confused with God, my private, gentler *Yahweh*, a deity who would never destroy the world with flood or banish anyone from Paradise. I had trouble imagining him as *a Romeo*—although I had no trouble imagining him as an innocent boy on horseback in an Autumn field being teased by buxom farmgirls, one of whom—according to my grandfather's favorite story—took the key to his childish treasure box, a key he wore on a string around his neck, and dropped it down her dress between her breasts.

"I went after it," my grandfather said simply. "What I found was better than the key."

Maybe, he *had* been a Romeo, after all.

Usually, when my grandfather came to this part of the story, my grandmother would throw up her hands with an exclamation, and my grandfather, giving her a sideways look, would ask if I wanted to see the medals and coins that had been in his box, treasures he had brought with him from the Old World. He would get the box—not the original box, now a red-and-gold container that used to hold tea—and I would study the contents: shiny coins with double-headed eagles, one old gray coin that looked as if a mouse had nibbled at its edge, a medal struck to commemorate the wedding of King George III of England . . . My grandfather never explained how he got the treasures. I never asked. Maybe he had gotten them from his father, who had gotten them from the count.

On the night—it was by now dawn—I hitchhiked to my grandparents' house, my grandfather brought out the box of treasures. And, then, since it was the day he went to the markets to buy groceries, meat, and fish for his store, he left the kitchen to get dressed. I sat up with my grandmother and, for the first time, asked her about what her life had been like in Plissa.

She had always talked about coming to America, working in a sweatshop in New York, buying books by Dickens and Zola, bringing them back to Russia to start a school for Jewish girls, getting caught in St. Petersburg during the Revolution, and walking through the Winter Palace the morning after the Reds had taken it over.

But she'd never talked about her childhood.

That morning I got a clue why.

"*Why* did Ruth spit at the Handsome Soldier?" my grandmother repeated my question. But didn't answer it. I don't think she had an answer. I had a feeling— improbable as it was—she'd never asked it herself. It simply was what had happened—the soldier raised Ruth's face, and she'd spit at him. And he'd raped her.

My grandmother didn't talk about the details of the rape—what he did, what Ruth did. She said she remembered the Bear telling the Handsome Soldier to hurry up. They were late. And she remembers the Soldier-on-Horseback looking away from the rape and smoking his pipe. She wanted to look away, too, but couldn't.

"It must have been horrible for you!" my sister, Bea, said to my grandmother, a few weeks later when she heard the story.

My grandmother shrugged. Pogroms, cholera, sweatshops, revolution, the Depression, two still-births, two world wars, the Holocaust, Korea, the Cuban Missile Crisis, Kennedy's assassination, the threat of nuclear annihilation, Vietnam, hippies fucking in public in Roger Williams Park . . .

"Life is hard," my grandmother said.

If a man find a damsel that is a virgin, that is not betrothed, and lay hold on her, and lie with her; and they be found; then the man that lay with her shall give unto the damsel's father fifty shekels of silver, and she shall be his wife, because he has humbled her; he may not put her away all his days. Deuteronomy 22: 28–29.

A man who rapes a virgin *na'arah*—a girl from twelve to twelve-and-a-half—must pay the fine and compensation for suffering.

A man who rapes a virgin *bogeret*—a girl over the age of twelve-and-a-half—does not have to pay the fine, but he must pay compensation for suffering, for pain, and—in the words of *The Torah Anthology*, a Ladino commentary on the Scripture—*for the reduction in her "value," since a virgin is more desirable than a woman who is not a virgin.*

According to the *Talmud*, Rav Yosef says the fine of fifty shekels is paid for the rape of a girl, not from *twelve* to twelve-and-a-half, but from *three* to twelve-and-a-half.

Ruth was a virgin *na'arah*. She had just turned twelve.

When my grandmother first told me the story, I had imagined Ruth to be older, a young woman—either because to my grandmother's six-year-old eyes she seemed to be grown up or because, in 1880 in a Lithuanian *shtetl*, a twelve-year-old girl was older than a twelve-year-old in Springfield or Providence in 1963.

Once I learned—from Bea—that Ruth was twelve, *younger*, not *older* than I was, *six years younger*, a kid, the rape seemed even more violent, the Handsome Soldier seemed more brutal.

On reading these pages, my ex-wife looked up at this point and accused me of sexism.

"*Why* is the rape of a young woman less brutal than the rape of a twelve-year-old?" she asked.

"Jewish law differentiates between a *na'arah* and a *bogeret*," I said.

"Jewish law also says don't eat shellfish," my ex-wife said. "What did you have for lunch?"

"Lobster," I admitted.

"You don't go to temple," my ex-wife said. "You don't keep kosher. You don't wear a *yarmulke*."

"I was describing what I felt in 1963, when I was eighteen," I said.

"Do you *still* think Ruth's rape was more brutal because she was twelve?" my ex-wife asked.

When I thought Ruth had been a young woman, I imagined her as tall as the Handsome Soldier, looking him in the eye as she spit into his face, someone who could have put up a struggle, scratched, punched, or kneed him . . .

When I imagined Ruth as a twelve-year-old, I saw a small girl, frail, with fragile wrists, someone who had to stretch up, perhaps on tiptoe, to spit into the Handsome Soldier's face, someone he could have lifted under the arms like an affectionate uncle and carried, helpless, into the woods, someone crushed under his greater weight . . .

Jewish tradition recognizes that in both cases—women and children—rape is an act of violence. But, in the case of a woman, rape violates her dignity. In the case of a child, rape violates innocence itself.

My ex-wife is troubled by the distinction. In 1963, my sister responded not to Ruth's age, but only to the rape—and its effect on my grandmother: *It must have been horrible for you!* My grandmother also made no mention of Ruth's age. Her stoicism seemed to acknowledge only the facts: *Rapes happen.* She shared none of my sentimentality, Bea's horror, or Maxie's idealism. Her practicality was rooted in an understanding of life Maxie, Bea, and I lacked—an understanding we resisted: Evil exists. Ruth could be raped. My grandfather Moses could murder and perhaps be murdered. My father could be an adulterer. My mother could go mad.

II

When my great-grandfather—Yitzchak—learned that his daughter Ruth had been raped, he left the house and slaughtered every animal he owned that was without blemish: a dozen chickens, a goat, two lambs, a cow . . . Then—according to Plissa's *yisker-bikher*, the town's memorial book—bloody to the elbows, Yitzchak walked to Polotsk, to the officers' training school, where he explained that one of the soldiers had raped his daughter. He demanded to talk to the commanding officer—who refused to see him.

The blood caked on his skin, Yitzchak raised his fist to the sky and, like a Moses in Pharaoh's court, called down God's curse on the commanding officer: Just as his— Yitzchak's—first child, his daughter, had been violated, so would the commanding officer's first child, male or female, be violated.

The commanding officer was superstitious. And Yitzchak's echo of Moses's threat was not lost on him. Even though he had no children, he was engaged to be married. The thought of his child being born under a curse made him uneasy. He had been brought up on stories about how Jews used the blood of Christian infants to make their unleavened bread. And he'd heard that Jewish sorcerers could foretell the future, raised the dead with Kabbalistic spells, and punished their enemies with the Evil Eye, causing mysterious rashes, and fits of laughing or weeping.

That night, the commanding officer woke from a nightmare. Calling out to an aide, he left orders that the crazy Jew, if he returned, should be shown in right away.

The next day, when Yitzchak—who had not washed and was still encrusted with dried blood—again demanded to see the commanding officer, the aide brought him in. But the sun was shining, the nightmare seemed no more than what it had been—a dream—and the commanding officer was embarrassed to have his men know he'd changed his mind about talking to the Jew. So he told the aide that there had been a misunderstanding. Under no circumstances would he receive the Jew.

Again, Yitzchak cursed the commanding officer's first-born.

And, again, that night, the commanding officer woke from a nightmare, called in his aide, and told him that he would see the Jew the following day. He was sure Yitzchak would return.

But, in the daylight, the commanding officer once more regretted his nighttime vow; and, when the aide brought Yitzchak in, the commanding officer once more pretended that the aide had misunderstood his orders.

Under no circumstances—the commanding officer said—would he talk to this Jew.

From the courtyard, Yitzchak saw the commanding officer standing at a window, watching.

The commanding officer may have felt like Pharaoh, but Yitzchak no longer felt like Moses.

Defeated, Yitzchak walked home to Plissa, stopping on the way to wash off the dried blood.

For the next week, the commanding officer suffered from nightmares. He grew pale from lack of sleep and thin from lack of appetite. Even in daylight, he swore he would meet with the Jew—who, however, seemed to be punishing him by *not* returning to demand an interview. The commanding officer became convinced that his firstborn would be cursed. And he developed a hatred for the crazy Jew who had given up so easily, leaving the commanding officer no chance to redeem himself and remove the curse.

Hatred turned into anger. Anger turned into action. With a dozen friends, the commanding officer galloped into Plissa, determined to kill as many Jews, young and old, as he could. Revenge for the child not yet born who was cursed . . .

It was one of the first pogroms that were to sweep the country during the following year, most sparked by the assassination of Alexander II and led by radicals who were convinced the violence was the beginning of a revolution that would topple the tsarist regime.

By dawn, a dozen Jews lay dead in the street. And three houses and two barns had been burned to the ground.

Coming out from hiding, Ruth looked at the carnage and went mad, tearing her clothes and hair and falling on first one body, then another, caressing it, mimicking the motions of copulation. Even though the town would not get the details of what led to the massacre until later, Ruth was convinced she was responsible for the tragedy.

Although, unwillingly and little by little, my grandmother told us most of what happened, she refused to say what eventually happened to Ruth.

"But if you don't tell us what happened," I said, "no one will know."

My grandmother said, "No one should know."

III

I had been insistent enough in my demands for information that, shortly before I left for college, my father took me for a walk to tell me to lay off my grandmother. My questions upset her.

"Why do you want to know this stuff anyway?" my father wondered.

I couldn't answer him—although I probably wouldn't have continued to be as aggressive in trying to draw out the information if it hadn't been for a German refugee— Hermann Keitel—an ex-Nazi I met through my high school girlfriend, Eva.

Eva—named for Eva Braun, Hitler's mistress—had come to Springfield three years earlier from a small town in Bavaria, where her grandfather, a local industrialist, ruled as if the Nazis had won the war. She never knew her father, a French occupation soldier who had raped her mother. Blond and blue-eyed, Eva had been brought up as an Aryan princess.

Why we got together—the granddaughter of a unrepentant Nazi and the son of a Jewish Trotskyist—is too obvious to examine, although at the time neither of us thought much about it.

In fact, the only time it came up was when we went to see *The Longest Day*, and I realized Eva was rooting for the guys with the subtitles.

We didn't avoid talking about World War II and the Holocaust. It just didn't seem relevant to our romance— even though two or three times a week, when we'd walk home from school together, we'd stop for tea at Keitel's apartment on Longhill Street.

Keitel was a distant relative of Field Marshall William Keitel, who, in August 1939, had tried to convince Hitler of the superiority of the Western powers and the danger

Germany would face in a general war and who, in July 1944, helped Hitler out of the *Lagbaracke* at Rastenburg after Count von Stauffenberg tried to assassinate Hitler with a bomb.

Keitel shuffled around his small room, which was filled with books and magazines, in scuffed loafers without socks, the pants from an old, elegant suit, and a cardigan sweater over a yellowing white shirt. His hair and eyebrows, like his shirt, were a stained white, the color of heavy cream. The pupils of his eyes were small and dark, almost black. His lips were pale. His English, learned when he was a boy, was good. In fact, he sounded more like a retired school teacher from England than a former member of the German army.

What he did in the war, he refused to reveal. He said he was ashamed to admit it in his adopted country.

"We"— he meant the Nazis —"were idealists," he said. "We *believed* . . . How else could we have done the horrible things we did?"

He felt betrayed by Hitler and read from Martin Bormann's book, *Hitler's Table-Talk*:

"I find it unpleasant when a car splashes mud on people lined up on the edge of the road," Hitler said on January 24, 1942, "especially when they're people in their Sunday clothes."

"*This* from a man who murdered millions!" Keitel said.

"Probably none of us is entirely 'normal,'" Hitler told Bormann on December 28, 1941. "Otherwise we should spend all our days in the cafe on the corner. The Catholics, the bourgeois, everyone has accused me of being crazy because, in their eyes, a normal man is one who drinks three glasses of beer every evening. 'Why all this fuss? It's obviously the proof that he's mad.' How many men of our Party were regarded in their families as black sheep!"

Keitel slammed the book shut.

"Black sheep," he muttered, "black sheep . . . The black sheep all followed the black shepherd . . ."

Keitel was writing a book about Walter Rathenau, a German Jew who urged complete assimilation, an economic visionary who, in his books, argued for international cooperation and individual freedom and who synthesized technology and transcendentalism—a liberal vision of the marriage of rationalism and mysticism that, perverted, fed National Socialism.

After World War I, Rathenau helped negotiate reparations. In 1922, he was chosen Minister of Reconstruction for the new Weimar Republic, an unpopular choice. His fellow industrialists hated him for his economic views. Nationalists hated him for his internationalism. Anti-Semites hated him because he was a Jew. Jews hated him because he was an assimilationist.

On June 24, 1922, he was assassinated.

"If Rathenau had lived," Keitel told me, "there would have been no Hitler, no National Socialism, no World War . . ."

Keitel thought Rathenau was a prophet and compared him to Moses, to Jesus. For hours, he would read from Rathenau's books as Eva and I sat in his small, cluttered room, which smelled of cigars, Jasmine tea, and, for some reason, damp wool, dust motes making shafts of late afternoon sun look like cloudy tubes of light. Impatient with his lectures, I'd stare at Eva and imagine us making love in the back of my parents' station wagon—which we did Saturday nights after going to the movies, although, embarrassed by how small her breasts were, Eva would never take off her blouse.

Two weeks before I left for college, I met Eva in Springfield's George Walter Vincent Smith's Museum, where we sometimes necked in the huge, usually empty gallery that held reproductions of famous statues—the Discus Thrower, the Emperor Augustus, with his blind egg-shell eyes, Praxiteles' *Hermes Carrying the Infant Dionysus*, whose naked body Eva said aroused her, and Aphrodite, whose marble— or was it plaster—body aroused me . . . Making out among the sculpture was like being at an orgy that had started over two thousand years ago.

But that summer afternoon I didn't feel romantic. It was the day after my father had told me to stop questioning my grandmother about her childhood—about Ruth's rape. I was confused, unhappy, angry. I didn't want to cause my grandmother distress, but I felt like I was being cheated.

Kids always want to know adult secrets. And part of my reaction was the same frustration I used to feel when my mother and father spoke Yiddish to each other to keep me and my sister from understanding. But, at least in retrospect, I think I also felt cheated on behalf of any children I would have—as surely as if my grandparents were wasting a family fortune, a legacy I wanted to pass on to future generations.

Eva and I left the museum and walked toward my house, the same route we used to take after school. The late summer air was heavy, hot. We were sweating. Both our shirts were damp around the armpits and along our spines.

When we crossed a street, the asphalt was soft. Windows were open in houses we passed—air conditioning was still a luxury—and we heard a radio broadcasting a baseball game, someone practicing a piano, a telephone ringing . . . From a distance came the drone of cars on Route 91, which mixed with the high-pitch churr of cicadas and an airplane passing overhead. The city felt empty like a restaurant after closing time.

"Do you think *we'll* ever have children?" Eva asked me. The next Fall, we were going to different schools. Neither of us admitted it, but we knew our romance was about to end. We were looking forward to the pleasure of being heartbroken.

Out of habit, we wandered up Longhill Street and stopped at Keitel's apartment. It was the last time I saw him.

Eva told Keitel what was bothering me.

"Make them tell you," he said. "You have to become their memory. Don't let anything be forgotten. The present disappears. The future doesn't exist. All we have is the past . . ."

And, finally, he told me what he had done in the war.

"I worked with Dr. Hermann Pfannmuller," Keitel said. "He ran an asylum near Munich. We took care of retarded children—*Ballastexistenzen*, living burdens . . . Pathetic little boys and girls, who just . . . weren't normal. Living burdens . . . I helped with the euthanasia program. We starved the children to death."

Keitel took my hand.

"Make them tell you," he repeated. "Make them tell you everything."

What happened to Ruth?

When my great-grandfather Yitzchak saw her pretending to copulate with the corpses of the Jews murdered in the pogrom, he, too, went momentarily mad and, trying to stop Ruth, strangled her.

 *five*

I

When my grandfather's father—Nathan or Nanie—was born, with his first breath, he cried out *Adonai*, the sacred name of God. Or so the story goes. Everyone assumed he would become a rabbi. And, early on, Nathan proved to be a prodigy. By the time he was seven, he was able to argue particulars of Talmudic law—according to a memoir by his contemporary and friend, the poet and journalist Judah Leib Gordon, who was also my grandmother Bella's great-uncle.

By the time Nathan was twelve, he had memorized the *Pentateuch* and much of the *Talmud* and *Mishna*. He was, everyone said, another Rabbi Elijah Zalman, the *Gaon* of Vilna, who was considered the most remarkable scholar to appear among the Jews in five hundred years. And Nathan's father, Moses, sent the boy to study with one of the *Gaon's* disciples, who—like the *Gaon*—emphasized Hebrew over Yiddish, the *Jerusalem Talmud* over the *Babylonian Talmud,* and included in the curriculum mathematics, history, geography, astronomy, anatomy, botany, and even music, subjects never taught in the *heders*.

Nathan's teacher—who came to Plissa from Galicia, during the famine of 1820—was also influenced by the *Haskalah,* the Jewish Enlightenment, which in Vilna in the early part of the nineteenth century, centered around a new synagogue, the *Taharat ha-Kodesh,* and its founder, Mordecai Aaron Guenzburg. Guenzburg was the headmaster of a Jewish school, which was modeled on principles set forth a generation earlier by Moses Mendelssohn. At Guenzburg's school, Nathan took additional courses, including German and French. Nathan taught himself Polish and Russian. By the time Nathan was sixteen, he had abandoned the *Talmud* for Goethe and Voltaire, Heine and Rousseau, Lessing and Pushkin.

Gordon approved of Nathan's enthusiasm for Goethe, who as a young man had helped put out a fire in the Frankfurt ghetto despite catcalls from Christians who watched, for Rousseau, who demanded equal rights for Jews and supported the idea of a Jewish state, and for Lessing, whose tolerance both Gordon and Nathan found exhilarating. Both Gordon and Nathan were interested in Islam and Palestine. And, in 1853, in letters, both expressed intense admiration for Abraham Mapu's *Ahavat Ziyyon—The Love of Zion—*the first modern Hebrew novel. They liked the book's Biblical settings, its heroism and emotion, and its emphasis on freedom.

Gordon, however, took a dim view of Nathan's passion

for Voltaire, whose attacks on religion included slurs on the Old Testament, for Heine, who was critical of his co-religionists, and for Pushkin—or rather Pushkin's creation, Eugene Onegin—whom Gordon dismissed as a *poseur*. In reading of Gordon's contempt for Onegin, it seems that Gordon is transferring his antagonism from his friend to a safer target.

Gordon describes Nathan as imagining himself another Onegin and, like his hero, seeking to "provoke the smile of ladies with the fire of unexpected epigrams." The lines Gordon quotes, in Russian—I'm quoting from Nabokov's translation—follow a damning portrait of Onegin and, presumably, also of Nathan:

> All of us had a bit of schooling
> in something and somehow:
> hence education, God be praised,
> is in our midst not hard to flaunt.
> Onegin was, in the opinion of many . . .
> a learned fellow but a pedant.

Gordon is also caustic about Nathan's admiration for Napoleon, whom Nathan worshipped as a liberator—a hurricane leveling superstition and old-fashioned customs. According to Gordon's memoir, they had rancorous fights in which Gordon attacked the Emperor for the Infamous Decrees of 1808, limiting the activities of Jews in the Eastern Provinces, and Nathan defended Napoleon for freeing Jews in France, Italy, and the German states. Gordon—in his book—dismisses Nathan's contention by claiming that Napoleon's acts, like Scripture, could be quoted to prove anything.

Nathan's father, Moses, was a moderate Jew, modern enough to wear his caftan short, but traditional enough to deplore the *maskilim*, the liberals with their pro-German ways, whom he dismissed contemptuously as *Deytshen* or *Berliners*. He was in favor of emancipation, but opposed to the assimilation necessary to bring emancipation about. He was proud of his son's achievement, but worried about the effect a secular education would have on him.

As a child, Nathan loved listening to the peddlers passing through town with stories of Court Jews, who dressed and acted like gentiles. As a young man, he grilled travelers about the New Spirit among Jews in the big cities of Germany and Russia. He read Raphael Fuerstenthal's secular Hebrew monthly *Ha-Me'assef*. And, to his father's disappointment but not surprise, in 1853, when he was twenty-three, Nathan announced that he was rejecting his calling—he would not be a rabbi. He was leaving home.

Not only was he leaving home, he was abandoning the faith of his ancestors. He wrapped his *talis* and *phylacteries* in cloth, put them in a box, and, instead of taking them with him, stuck the box on a shelf.

When Nathan reached Warsaw, he wrote home. The only letters to survive—in fragments—appear in Gordon's memoirs, with references to other, troubled letters to Nathan's family. Apparently, Nathan's father had either withheld his blessing or, worse, cursed Nathan—Gordon's account is unclear.

Nathan's letter refers to the traditional blessing given to a son about to leave on a trip: a father laying his hand on the son's head and saying, "May God make thee like Ephraim and Manasseh," followed by the priestly benediction from *Numbers*, "The Lord bless thee, and keep thee; the Lord lift up His countenance upon thee, and give thee peace."

"I survived the heavy hand on my head," Nathan wrote. "My own could not have been heavier."

Perhaps, Nathan blessed—or cursed—himself.

My grandfather's brother—Heschel, *Harry*—used to tell a version of Nathan's departure in which Nathan's father, Moses, compared himself to Isaac, saying that Isaac used his blindness as an excuse to bless his second son, Jacob, instead of his firstborn, Esau.

According to Heschel, Moses said he wished *he* were blind, so *he* could pretend to be ignorant of his son's apostasy.

In his memoirs, Gordon—referring to the paternal blessing—says, "Ephraim and Manasseh were both born in Egypt. Their mothers were daughters of Egyptian priests, so by the laws of . . . matriarchy neither were Jews— although both, adopted by Jacob, became ancestors of one of the Twelve Tribes."

Nathan never reached Berlin.

After leaving Warsaw, he was attacked by a band of Jewish *catchers*, thugs who shanghaied young men and boys—*Poimaniki*, the captured recruits—to fill the Jewish quota for the Russian army.

For the next seven years, no one in Plissa heard from or about Nathan. He was presumed dead.

II

In the Fall of 1863, Nathan returned to Plissa. He arrived at night, traveling by foot, hungry, sick with a fever, and fearful. He had deserted the army the previous Spring and had been trying to get home ever since. His face was scarred by a white ridge—a saber cut—from forehead to chin, across his nose and his mouth, which was permanently twisted by the wound into a sardonic grin. When he took a bath, his father saw that his back was also scarred—so badly puckered the healed flesh looked like tree bark.

With Nathan was another deserter, a friend, a radical, named Nikolai Solbetsky, a gentile from Cieszanow, a town about fifty miles northeast of Minsk, which, in 1856, had a population of 3,337—2,226 Jews and only 1,111 gentiles.

Gordon calls him Solbetsky. But in Arthur Rackwick's *Letters from the Crimean War, 1854–56*, Rackwick, an American journalist, refers to a Nikolai Subetsky from Cieszanow, who was "drunk and abusive one night in the Casino." The Casino was probably the Sebastapol Club, which during the siege was used for a time as an infirmary.

Rackwick described Subetsky as a Polish aristocrat, who bragged about his descent, on his mother's side, from Stephan Bathody, the Prince of Transylvania, described in the *Encyclopedia Britannica*, Eleventh Edition, as a man of "genius and valor." Elected by the *szlachta*, the senate, Bathody briefly reigned after Henry of Valois, a liberal king imported from France on the death of Siegismund II, bolted at midnight, June 18, 1574, for his homeland.

According to family legend, Subetsky or Solbetsky, as Gordon—and my grandfather's brother, Heschel—called him, also was distinctly related to the Czartoryscys, who were, from the middle 1700s to the early 1800s, sort of Polish Kennedys, brothers who attempted to centralize and strengthen the state at the expense of the power of the conservative ruling class—the Potoccy, the Radzillowie, and the Lubomirscy—whose individual estates were semi-independent fiefdoms.

According to Gordon's memoirs, Solbetsky's father had fought in the unsuccessful Polish uprising of 1830 against Russia and had either gone into exile, been deported to Siberia or Orenburg, or been killed. His estate—according to Gordon—was confiscated.

But Rackwick reports Solbetsky—or Subetsky—bragged that, rather than let his estate fall into the hands of "cringing and greasy Jews," his father divided the land among the peasants—although, at the time, it is unlikely that Jews could have owned an estate, since property was valued by the number of souls who lived on the land and it was inconceivable for a Jew to own a Christian soul.

In either case, Subetsky—or Solbetsky—was raised in genteel poverty, his bloodline richer than his income.

III

Whether or not Nathan's Solbetsky was Rackwick's Subetsky, the Polish radical and deserter who accompanied

Nathan to Plissa had met Nathan during the Crimean War. Heschel's account of their meeting is simple.

Sometime during the five days after the battle at Balaklava and before the battle of Inkerman, Solbetsky insulted Nathan by refusing to drink in the same room with him—probably a tavern. During the battle of Inkerman, Solbetsky ran away from the fighting. Nathan either followed him or found him—stumbling on him, *over* him, in the cannon smoke, which, heavy as a fog, obscured the battlefield.

The conflict was "a melee," according to one account, "a true soldiers' battle," according to another. The Russians left 12,000 men on the field, which the anonymously published *The Crimea: A Surgeon's Journal* described as being calf-deep in mud and blood, men and horses looming out of the smoke, faces contorted . . . The first cannonball the surgeon heard "whistled like a tea kettle." The second, following right after the first, sounded louder, "like the whistle of a train." The third was silent—or rather the anonymous surgeon noticed no sound except the thud as the cannonball struck near him, "plowing up the field." The sunset through the smoke was the most beautiful the surgeon had ever seen. When he turned over one fallen soldier with his foot, the body rolled, the head, severed, did not.

Although the battle was tragic, Heschel's account is farce.

Terrified, Solbetsky—and *this* detail Heschel told with malicious glee—had lost control of his bowels. (Heschel loved scatological stories. One of his other favorite anecdotes—about his experiences in World War I—

involved taking pot-shots at a German soldier, who kept creeping out of his trench to relieve his bowels. Heschel would wait until the German had dropped his pants and squatted, before shooting over the soldier's head and sending him scuttling back into the trench. This game went on—according to Heschel—for over an hour. And Heschel hoped that he had left the poor soldier with a case of constipation that lasted until the armistice.) At great risk, Nathan helped Solbetsky, who was paralyzed by fear and shame, to get to safety. Heschel claims Nathan carried Solbetsky off the battlefield, in the process smearing himself with Solbetsky's feces.

After Inkerman, Solbetsky again publicly insulted Nathan—although how or where is unclear—and kept insulting him, trying to provoke a fight, probably to prove to Nathan that he, Solbetsky, was not a coward. Nathan refused to take the bait. When Nathan backed down, Solbetsky ridiculed Nathan, accusing *him* of cowardice.

Later—hours later? days later? weeks later?—Solbetsky privately confronted Nathan and asked him why Nathan hadn't fought. Because of Nathan's behavior on the battlefield, Solbetsky knew Nathan was brave. Why had Nathan let people think him a coward?

"Because," Nathan said, "if we had fought, I would have had to kill you."

After that, Heschel claimed, they became unlikely friends.

The story—like a stone smoothed by years of handling—has a polish that makes me distrust its accuracy. But, whatever happened at Inkerman, by the time Nathan and Solbetsky arrived at Plissa, they *had* become friends.

Together, Nathan and Solbetsky had deserted the Russian army, following the Polish uprising of 1863. A battle between Polish patriots and Russian troops took place the first week of May, in the woods of Kobylanka, near Cieszanow, Solbetsky's home. Nathan and Solbetsky traveled there by foot, arriving two weeks after the fighting— which was, according to W. H. Bullock's *Polish Experiences During the Insurrection of 1863–1864*, worse than that of the Battle of Fredericksburg during the American Civil War.

"The [Polish] cavalry was not stopped by the marsh, but, in the face of the guns planted on the other side, rode boldly into it. The Russian gunners seeing this, at once took flight, and had not the cavalry become hopelessly entangled in the marsh, the two guns might have been captured . . ."

The 1,500 Russians were driven back by only 300 Poles "whose ammunition was quite exhausted."

"The ground . . . was saturated with blood when I passed the day after the fight. From the pocket of one dead Russian we took a packet containing opium. Gloves, boots, bottles, bread, caps, coats, drawers, wooden spoons, were strewn all about the wood, and the trees were cut to pieces by cannon-balls, canister shot, and bullets. Especially in the centre of the insurgent camp, near the general's quarters, where I had passed two nights, the trees were literally shivered to atoms . . ."

At sunset, between engagements, Bullock heard "the cuckoo and the turtle doves," which might "at any moment be drowned by the din of battle . . ." Sounds that Nathan and Solbetsky probably also heard when they arrived on the scene, after the Polish retreat, where they also probably saw—like Bullock—in the marshes, "the carcasses of men and horses . . . putrefying."

IV

A photograph taken of Nathan's youngest sister, Gittel, shortly before the turn of the century in London, when she was in her sixties, shows a woman who looks like a sixteen-year-old aged by stage makeup. A round face with eyes squinting in merriment and skin the texture of crumpled silk. "She didn't walk," Gordon wrote in his memoirs, "she skipped"—like one of the legendary *Children of Joy*, who were created out of God's laughter when, on the Eighth Day, He looked on His Creation with delight.

When Solbetsky met Gittel, the night he and Nathan arrived in Plissa, he—according to Gordon—called her *the rain-charm girl*. In Slavic mythology, *the rain-charm girl*, nude and covered with garlands, twirls in the middle of a circle, singing prayers to the sky to bring on the showers, which would fructify the land. Solbetsky said— Gordon reports—that Gittel's clothes smelled of flowers, unlike all the (presumably Christian) girls he knew, whose clothes smelled of Church incense.

Solbetsky wooed Gittel with tales of the Knights of the Sword and of how, centuries ago, in a forest in Galicia, the infant Jesus led Casimir the Great away from a Russian ambush. He told her about how innocent Pandora opened the casket, which was the last gift of the gods, and let loose into the world pain, sickness, terror, grief, death—and, finally, hope. And how the giant Prometheus took pity on the frail creatures—man and woman—and gave them the gift of fire, for which he was punished by being chained to the Caucasus Mountains, where a vulture eternally gnawed at his heart. He recited Anton Malczewski's Byronic poem *Marya* and, in English, Browning's *Any Wife to Any Husband*, part of which Gordon recorded in his memoirs:

> And if a man would press his lips to lips
> Fresh as the wilding hedge-rose-cup there slips
> The dew-drop out of, must it be by stealth?

Gittel resisted Solbetsky's stories with stories of her own: How the Recording Angel Metratron fell in love with a maiden from Slonim, took her away from her family, and lifted her up to Heaven, where he kept her captive until she guessed all of his seventy names. How the Lord God gave King Solomon a flying carpet made of green silk with gold embroidery. How Solomon had a trained cat who sat on its hind paws and held up a candle to light the King's supper. And how the letter Yod caused Asmodeus, king of the demons, to take the form of Solomon and to sleep with all the King's wives. Gittel told Solbetsky about how Queen Esther tricked the wicked Prime Minister of Persia Haman into barking like a dog. And how the Czar of Russia once saw a Jewish woman milking a goat and was so taken by her beauty that he asked her to marry him.

I cannot marry you, the woman, who was very pious, said.

I will sit you beside me on my throne and half of my kingdom will be yours.

I cannot marry you, the woman repeated.

The Czar ordered the woman to marry him.

The woman said, *If I must, I must. But, first, there is something about me you should know. I cannot die. When you are an old man, I will still be young. I cannot die . . .*

The Czar was skeptical.

But the woman said, *I will prove it.*

She told one of the Czar's guards to stab her in the heart with his saber. The guard looked at the Czar.

It's all right, the woman said. *I cannot die.*

The Czar nodded at the guard, who plunged his saber into the woman's heart. The woman died instantly—thereby protecting her virtue.

Gittel parried every story Solbetsky told with one of her own—day after day, as if they were in a duel. And with every passing day, Solbetsky's love grew.

He confided in Gordon that what he loved about Gittel most were her hands, which had something blunt, unformed about the fingers, pudgy child's hands, reaching, clutching, grasping flowers, bread, beads, cloth, life, Solbetsky's back as she kissed him in the yard while her brother Nathan looked on from his sickbed near a loft window.

Despite his fever, Nathan stumbled down the stairs and out into the yard, where, scaring the chickens, he attacked Solbetsky, beating him until Solbetsky was almost dead.

When Nathan, drenched in sweat from the fight and his fever, stood up and looked down at Solbetsky's bloody face, Nathan said, *This is the third time I've saved your life.*

And the last. I should have killed you. And, if I ever see you again, I will.

That night, Solbetsky left Plissa—with Gittel, who married him when they reached Warsaw. And who converted to the Orthodox Church.

V

After Solbetsky and Gittel fled, Nathan became silent, solitary. *He* had left Plissa. *He* had brought the gentile back. *He* was responsible for Gittel's disgrace.

The family sat *shiva* for Gittel—who was considered dead. But, after a time, everyone got used to Gittel's absence.

Everyone except Nathan.

When Nathan recovered from his fever, from morning to night, he walked in the fields. He came back with so many burrs stuck to his trouser legs, he looked like his legs had sprouted wiry hair. He looked like a faun. At home, he was sullen. He'd sit, staring into the fire without moving for hours. Gordon tried to talk to him, but Nathan turned on his old friend angry eyes, eyes—Gordon wrote —*blazing like a prophet's* and Gordon withdrew.

Nathan's mother, at a loss, secretly consulted a local wise woman, who whispered that Nathan was possessed by a demon, one of the spirits born of Eve's copulation with the Serpent, *an emanation of the left side.*

Such demons, male and female, long for intercourse with humans, the wise woman said.

By spending so much time among the *goyim*, Nathan

had rendered himself vulnerable to the demon's seductions. His silence was—according to the wise woman—evidence of Nathan's struggle with temptation.

Like Saul, who, as the Scripture tells, was also troubled by "an evil spirit from God," Nathan needed someone to distract him—as David distracted Saul by playing upon his harp and singing: ". . . so," as it says in *I Samuel*, "Saul found relief, and it was well with him, and the evil spirit departed from him."

You mean, Nathan's mother asked the wise woman, *we need to find a harpist?*

The wise woman gave Nathan's mother an amulet to put around Nathan's neck.

Nathan, disgusted with his mother's superstition, refused to wear the amulet. So, at night, while Nathan slept, secretly his mother sewed the amulet into the hem of Nathan's jacket.

When Nathan noticed the lump and found the amulet, he threw the whole jacket into the fire. Such prodigality convinced Nathan's mother that Nathan *was* in fact possessed.

Nathan's father, also at a loss, consulted a rabbi from Vilna, who, an enlightened scholar, dismissed the wise woman's theory of possession.

Demons rarely visit men today, the Rabbi from Vilna said. *The mazzikim, the demons, all left the world when Moses first erected the sanctuary in the desert.*

One night, the Rabbi from Vilna came to Plissa to visit Nathan, who as usual was brooding. In the corners of the room, among the cobwebs, the fire cast shadows that looked like wings, talons, and beaks . . .

The Rabbi from Vilna shooed everyone else out of the house. Then, he sat next to Nathan. He, too, stared into the fire.

Nathan's father and mother, brothers and sisters, uncles and aunts, cousins and friends peered into the room through the windows, their faces, illuminated by the firelight, pale as lanterns . . .

Nathan clasped his hands. The Rabbi from Vilna clasped *his* hands. Nathan crossed his legs. The Rabbi from Vilna crossed *his* legs. Nathan sighed. The Rabbi from Vilna sighed.

For two hours, they sat in silence.

Finally, Nathan, vexed, asked, *What do you want?*

The Rabbi from Vilna said, *Vodka.*

You came all this way for vodka? Nathan asked.

The Rabbi from Vilna shrugged.

Nathan stood, crossed the room, and got some vodka, which he gave to the Rabbi from Vilna. Then, Nathan again sat.

The Rabbi from Vilna gave Nathan a look.

What? asked Nathan, impatiently.

You're not drinking? the Rabbi from Vilna asked.

No, Nathan said.

The Rabbi from Vilna shrugged—and emptied the glass, which he held out for a refill, which Nathan grudgingly gave him. When the Rabbi from Vilna hesitated, Nathan snapped, *I'm not drinking!*

Once more, the Rabbi from Vilna shrugged and slugged back the vodka.

This time, when the Rabbi from Vilna held out the glass

for a refill, Nathan brought him the stone bottle, which held the vodka.

The Rabbi from Vilna drank—and told the story of the Fox and the Monkey.

One day, the Fox came to the Monkey's house and found the Monkey sitting in the middle of the floor, sobbing.

"What's the matter, brother?" the Fox asked.

The Monkey turned his tear-streaked face up to the Fox and said, "I'm weeping for the destruction of the Temple in Jerusalem. Weeping for the great tragedy of our people."

The Fox nodded.

"I understand," he said.

The Fox sat on the floor beside the Monkey and joined in the Monkey's lament.

Together, for hours, they wept. They cried so hard they became weak.

"I think," the Fox said, "that we need something to renew our strength. Do you have any *schnapps*?"

The Monkey brought out the bottle and poured them each a shot, which they drank. Immediately, they felt revived, and they resumed weeping.

But, after a little while, the Fox said, "If one drink makes us this strong, think of what two drinks will do!"

So they poured another round and drank. Immediately, they felt even better.

"Imagine," the Fox said, "how much better we'll feel with three drinks?"

By the time they had finished the bottle, they were so drunk they were singing and dancing, making such a racket that the Monkey's wife came into the room. She took one look at the two cavorting animals and asked, "What's going on?"

Without missing a dance step, the Monkey said, "We're lamenting the Destruction of the Temple in Jerusalem."

At the end of the story, Nathan nodded. He reached for the bottle of vodka and took a swig.

When the Rabbi from Vilna left—just after dawn the following morning—Nathan had stopped grieving for his runaway sister.

And he had taken out the *talis* and *tefilin* he had put away so many years before.

VI

Shortly after my father's bar mitzvah—at the orphanage— *his* father, my grandfather, showed up and slipped my father, as if it were a bottle of his bootleg whiskey, a *Megillah*, a scroll with the story of *Esther*, which *he* had gotten on *his* bar mitzvah from Nathan.

Decades later, I found it, in my father's study, behind a set of Dickens—a beaten metal tube containing a parchment scroll.

Embarrassed by it—or by the sentimentality implied by his saving it—my father, ardent Trotskyist and atheist that he was, refused to discuss it.

"I don't know what it's doing there," he said.

Not just a clue to the past. A smoking gun! I begged him to tell me more about it; but, infuriated by what seemed to him my reactionary impulse, my father uncharacteristically ordered me to put the *Megillah* back.

I refused.

My father sent me to my room without supper.

Twilight came. Through the opened window, I heard *The Great Gildersleeve, Our Miss Brooks, Henry Aldrich*— radio's version of reality, a world that seemed cozy, appealing with its hometown wholesomeness and zany neighbors, many of whom were minority stereotypes— black menials, Irish cops, Jewish shopkeepers, tight-fisted Scots, supercilious Englishmen, passionate Italians, dumb Swedes, cold-blooded Germans . . . America's commedia dell'arte citizens. Most of whom had traded in their pasts for a present as fleeting as a live radio broadcast.

That night, when my father came into my bedroom to say good night, he said, "If you drive with your eyes fixed on the rear-view mirror, you'll never stay on the road."

He was right, of course; but if you ignored the rear-view mirror, you might get blind-sided by something that was gaining on you.

I went to sleep, dreaming of a *shtetl* with thatched cottages, magic beans, and villagers shrewd enough to outwit the Devil (who, clown that he was, unsuccessfully tried to catch souls with a regularity that was pathetic). A scene that was as alien to the radio's 1950s American hometown as it was possible to get and that was drawn as much from Grimms' fairy tales as from the Sholom Aleichem stories I'd read.

In the middle of the night, I woke, famished.

I snuck to the head of the stairs and saw, down below, an oblong of light from the kitchen and heard strange chanting. I crept downstairs and peered around the edge of the door.

My father, barefoot, in pajamas and bathrobe, sat at the kitchen table, wearing Nathan's yarmulke, *talis*, and *tefilin*, and reading in perfect Hebrew from the unscrolled *Megillah*.

 *six*

I

The text of Nathan's story, I got from Gordon's memoir.
The sub-text, I got from Heschel, the only relative to talk
freely about our family's history; but, slyly inventive, he
was not an entirely trustworthy reporter.

He peopled his past with wolves that walked on hind
legs in the woods at night, watching him as he hurried
across the frozen ground to the outhouse, drunken counts,
cossacks who galloped through Plissa, waving vodka bottles
like sabers, sweet-smelling haystacks in which he, like his
brother—my grandfather—fumbled at the bodices of the
girls who rouged their cheeks with berry juice, itinerant
mystics whose red silk-lined capes flowed from their shoulders like flames, and revolutionaries with faces like wooden
Indians who would stop on their way from one sinister
rendezvous to another.

At night, when Heschel would sit on the edge of my bed in the spare room of his house in Providence, he'd conjure up the world of his childhood so vividly that today, forty years later, there are moments as I drift to sleep when my dreams are invaded by counts and cossacks and peasant girls, and I seem to be not in my bed but in Lithuania at the turn of the century.

In this vivid past, I get glimpses and echoes of what came before, hints from stray words about my ancestors like my great-grandfather, who one winter night when he was on the way to the outhouse was attacked by a wolf.

"He had to shit so bad, he didn't have time to be scared," Heschel said.

Barehanded, he strangled the beast.

The count who owned the estate on which Heschel and my grandfather grew up—the estate Nathan managed for many years after returning to Plissa—gave my great-grandfather a ring. Nathan got it—according to family legend—for trading outfits with the count when they were traveling through Russia. Why did they trade clothes? Where were they going?

In 1972, when—for reasons that are no longer clear to me, for fun, to shock—I shaved my head, I looked like a mongol peasant, the oriental hooding of the inner canthus of each eye more noticeable. Did this suggestion of the steppes come from ancestors who converted to Judaism? Or from some Kahalkhan or Buriat warrior who raped a Jewish woman?

This far back in my family's history, scenes— fragmentary and suggestive—are like half-finished museum exhibits. Mannikins with indistinct faces wearing a scrap of authentic cloth, using a bowl reconstructed from a single shard.

The *Megillah* I'd discovered was similar to one I saw at the Jewish Museum in New York, dating back over a thousand years and made in the Middle East. My grandfather claimed he once saw a lock of hair, since lost, which used to be tucked into the end of the scroll. *His* grandfather, my great-great-grandfather, told him it had belonged to Queen Esther herself, had been clipped from her head either by or for the Persian King Ahasuerus, Xerxes the Great, 2,500 years ago—an unlikely story.

But how did the story originate? How many generations back does that tale go? And whose hair was it?

Was the *Megillah* carried by Jews from some Middle Eastern desert into Eastern Europe? If so, when?

How much of the past do I carry with me, unknowingly? A few summers ago, on a visit to New Delhi, when other Westerners collapsed, exhausted by the 112-degree midday heat, I found myself striding through the city, energized by the sun.

"You must come from desert people," said the Indian I was with.

Perhaps some Semitic gene, long dormant, was triggered by the heat.

"Our history is old," Heschel would say after telling me stories of the past. "What we don't remember, we find in dreams."

I would dream of transcontinental migrations, Persian splendor, and deserts hammered by the sun.

After the 1800s, my family history is documented. Letters, photographs, memories of people who lived through the events they described . . . Imagination only fills in motivation or paints a backdrop or the scrim through which the action is seen. A gesture hinted at is described. The smell of tobacco smoke creates a pipe. A tune whistled in the night conjures up a man disappearing on a Lower East Side street.

Before 1800, there are fewer and fewer facts. I have to follow clues to my family history like Hansel following bread crumbs out of the forest. Or—perhaps—more like Theseus following Ariadne's thread out of the Labyrinth. The landscape changes.

The legends and myths that drift through the lives of my more recent ancestors may color in an outline. But the outline exists.

Did my grandfather, Moses, talk to God at Nisanoff's? If he did, I know enough about Moses to suspect that the conversation would have happened as the story describes it. The legend confirms Moses's character.

For forebears in the early nineteenth century and before, legends and myths don't corroborate character, they are the only things I know.

Like Jack on his beanstalk, I scramble up my family tree until I reach the kingdom in the clouds which is my own family's distant past.

II

In the month of Nisan, *the month of ripening barley*, 5556—1796—prodigies were seen in and around Plissa: wandering stars, a panther swimming in the Viliya River, a baby born with three nipples . . .

The following month, an epidemic, probably an influenza, killed dozens of Christians in Plissa. It may or may not have also killed Jews. But the Christians were convinced the Jews escaped and were, in fact, the cause of the disease.

Bereaved Christian fathers, husbands, and sons attacked the Jews of Plissa one dawn after a night of drinking. They slaughtered a Jewish child for every Christian child who died of the influenza, a Jewish mother for every Christian mother, a Jewish father for every Christian father . . .

By nightfall, when the Christians left, a silence fell over the town.

The Jews who survived were too frightened to weep. Wild pigs came out of the woods and trotted through the blood-soaked streets, rooting about the Jewish corpses, eating the flesh . . .

A month later, the night of the old moon, a stranger—an itinerant Jewish shoemaker, Isaac Laquedem—arrived in town with his sixteen-year-old daughter, Chana—Hannah—the most beautiful woman anyone had ever seen.

Hannah's skin was rose-tinted like the flesh of a radish. The fringe of hair, escaping from under her kerchief, was the red of current juice.

My great-great-grandfather, Nathan's father Moses, first saw Hannah when she and Isaac came to pay their respects to Moses's father, Yussel—Joseph. Moses was thirty-five years old, a widower, whose wife—Bella—had died in childbirth.

He wasn't embittered. But, in the years following the death of his wife, he showed no inclination to remarry. No interest in any of the local maidens—even his dead wife's younger sister, Gittel, whom everyone expected him to marry.

Which is why everyone was intrigued when Moses took an interest in Hannah.

Hannah sat in the courtyard behind Moses's father's house, glancing up from under her brow as she ate a boiled potato, peeling the skin with white, sharp, fox-like teeth.

Isaac was vague about where they came from.

In one conversation—with Moses's father—Isaac hinted that he'd been "in the East."

In another conversation—with Plissa's richest Jewish merchant—Isaac mentioned being recently in Brussels, Leipzig, and Munich . . .

Isaac's daughter, Hannah, told Moses that she and her father had just returned from Safed, a town in the mountains above the Hula Valley in Upper Galilee, an unearthly place, "the Jewish Shangri-la," where—it was rumored—the synagogue was painted blue; where cats, hundreds of cats, stared from the tops of ochre-colored stone walls, slinked through shadowed archways, and licked themselves in dusty lanes, all *gilgulim*, incarnations of dead mystics; and where Kabbalists, dressed in white with flowers in their hair, twirled like dervishes in the declining Sabbath sun.

Eighteen years earlier, in 1778, three hundred Hasidim, disciples of the Ba'al Shem Tov, had emigrated to Safed from Vitebsk. Fourteen years later, the disciples of the *Gaon* of Vilna, Enlightened antagonist of the Hasidim, would follow the disciples of the Ba'al Shem Tov to Safed.

"Why were you in Safed?" Moses asked Hannah, who answered, "Paying our respects at the grave of the *Ari*"—Isaac Luria, the greatest Kabbalist of all time.

"Why were you in Safed?" Moses asked Hannah's father, Isaac, who answered, "Studying the communal system of government," a socialistic experiment, modeled on the Essene tradition.

"Why were you in Safed?" the Rabbi and the richest merchant asked both Hannah and her father, who looked at each other and said, "We *weren't* in Safed."

"There's something wrong with them," the Rabbi told the merchant, who agreed, adding, "Lock up our money."

"Lock up our *sons*," said the Rabbi, who watched Hannah as she walked along the Niemiecka—*German Street*—every man mesmerized by the swaying of her hips.

"I want to marry your daughter," Moses told Isaac.

"Do you have wealth?" Isaac asked.

"No," Moses said.

"Do you have position in the community?" Isaac asked.

"I'm just a poor farm boy," Moses said.

"What can you offer my girl?" Isaac asked.

"Love," Moses said.

"Love, she can get from anyone," Isaac said. "What can you offer my girl?"

"My life," Moses said.

"The men of Plissa," Isaac said, "see how they gaze at my girl. Any one of them would give up his life for her. What can *you* offer my girl?"

"My soul," Moses said.

Isaac smiled—and, as in a fairy tale, told Moses that, to win Hannah, Moses had to undergo three trials.

"Once started on this test," Isaac said, "you may not quit."

Isaac had Moses swear, one hand on his testicles— *testify*—that he would do what had to be done no matter how odd, hard, or dangerous the tasks were.

The first task *was* odd. On the following Friday, just as the sun balanced on the horizon, Moses had to snip a lock from his hair.

Moses's half-brother, *Dovid*—David, for whom I was named—warned Moses: "The sun will be down. Don't violate the Sabbath."

"The sun won't be down," Moses said. "It won't be the Sabbath."

They asked the Rabbi, who said that, just before the sun went down, there *is* a moment that is neither day nor night, not Sabbath, but yet not *not* Sabbath, a moment when God blinks, which falls outside the Law, a time when the *Se'irim*, the hairy demons, copulate with virgins, when Angels pause in their praise of the Lord and listen to God's voice, which roars like silence, when the spirits of the dead consort with the spirits of those not yet born, when the *mekhashef*—sorcerers—work their wonders . . .

"There are rumors," David said.

Rumors that despite his age Isaac could stand on one hand, that he could do long arithmetical calculations in his head, that he sang so sweetly birds would fall silent to listen, that he spoke every known language—and, like Rabbi Hillel, some unknown languages: the language of the *shedim'*, the devils, the language of fire, the popping and hissing of burning logs, the language of the wind, the language of running water, the language of growing plants, the language of fever, the language of laughter, the language of *Lamashtu*, the hag who kills babies in the womb, the language of the Angels of the Presence—Michael, Gabriel, Raphael, and Phanuel—the language of Adam and Eve, which is like the growling of beasts, the language of the *'elohim*, which is the sound light makes at the break of day, the language of the Angel of Death, who is a fugitive, which is a sound that is no sound, the language of Noah, which is what Mankind spoke before God confused their tongues in Shinar at the Tower of Babel . . .

There were also rumors that, while in Rome, Isaac had read in the cards that he would end his days in a house under a black sun.

David pointed at a wooden sign over the doorway of a shop—a sun, so covered with grime it was black. The shop belonged to Simon Zunser, a goldsmith.

"Isaac must be a sorcerer," David warned.

"He's a cobbler," Moses said, "with a strange sense of humor."

"And Hannah may be a witch," David added. "Or a vampire."

At the ritual baths, one of the women thought she saw—on Hannah—a tiny tail.

"If her tail is as lovely as the rest of her," Moses said, "I'll be lucky indeed."

"If you win her," David said.

"I'll win her," Moses said.

Poised with the scissors, Moses watched the sun going

down, and just before sunset, he cut his hair—which, according to Isaac's instructions, he put under his bed that night.

In the middle of the night, Moses woke.

Hannah lay, in bed, naked, beside him. Her skin was as pale as rosewater; her red hair, radiant, like an ember. Moses caressed her, surreptitiously, checking to see if she had a tail. She didn't.

They made love until just before dawn, when Hannah whispered, "I must go."

As she slipped from the bed, Moses started after her.

"Stay here," Hannah said.

Still naked, she disappeared out the door into the dark street.

Moses fell back asleep.

He was awakened by excited voices. Half-a-dozen of the leading Jews of Plissa were passing the house, arguing.

Moses hurried outside, where David explained: The night before, a Christian was staggering home from a tavern, when he was waylaid by a giant, who had snapped his body in two as if it were a stick.

The victim had been the leader of the mob who had slaughtered the Jews the previous month.

That afternoon, Isaac gave Moses his second task, which was hard.

The following Friday, just before Sabbath, Moses had to dig a hole as deep as he was tall, toss in the lock of hair that he had cut off, and refill the hole, shoveling in the last clod of dirt the moment before sunset.

A moment too soon or a moment too late . . . failure.

"You must finish the very moment between day and night," Isaac said.

"Isaac is a *mekhashef*," David warned.

Solomon Meisel, the butcher, heard a voice speaking from Isaac's armpit, which the great Talmudist Rashi claimed was a sign of familiar spirits.

"A puny spirit to live in such a skinny, old man's armpit," Moses said.

"You joke," David said, "but Isaac wants to steal your soul."

"My soul," Moses said, "he doesn't have to steal. I will trade it happily for Hannah's love."

"Blasphemy!" David said. "*Vai iz mir!*"

Again, in the middle of the night, Moses woke. Again, Hannah lay, in bed, naked, beside him. In the moonlight, her skin was as silvery, as metallic as the scales of a fish and her hair as red as freshly slaughtered beef.

Again, they made love until just before dawn, when Hannah whispered, "I must go."

Again, naked, she got out of bed.

When Moses reached out to delay her, his hand passed through her body as if she were a ghost—although, after she left, Moses convinced himself that he had only imagined that his hand had passed through Hannah's body. The dim light must have played a trick on his eyes.

As before, Moses drifted off to sleep and was awakened by excited voices, talking about more murders.

The mysterious giant had attacked three Christians, a father and his two sons, who had been among the bloodiest killers during the previous month's pogrom.

"Every time we sleep together," Moses told Hannah, "someone dies."

Hannah avoided Moses's gaze, looking down and to the side.

"My father wants to give you your third test," she said. "After that, you and I will be as one."

Isaac was tramping through a field, collecting flowers, berries, and roots, his caftan starred with burrs.

"Every time Hannah comes to me," Moses said, "someone dies."

"Hannah has been coming to you?" Isaac said, digging up some *yo'ezer*—maidenhair fern—and putting it in a bag that hung from a sash around his waist.

Moses said nothing, watching as Isaac walked a few paces, searching the ground for more medicinal plants.

"*Yo'ezer* is good for the liver," Isaac said. "*Shihlayim*"—garden cress—"is good for the stomach."

"The sages tell us to depend on God's mercy," Moses said, "not herbs."

"Asaph ha-Yehudi wrote a book on medicine, the *Safer Asaf ha-Rofe*," Isaac said. "So did Solomon. And the Angel Raphael taught Noah how to cure diseases using tree bark, fruit, and roots."

"Why are people dying?" Moses said.

"People die all the time," Isaac said, stooping to dig up some wild garlic.

Moses grabbed Isaac and pulled him upright.

"Why are people dying?" he repeated.

"*Goyim* are dying," Isaac said, "not Jews."

"Unless you tell me why people are dying," Moses said, "I'm through with you."

"And with Hannah?" Isaac slyly asked.

Moses didn't answer.

Isaac smiled a secret smile.

"The third test," Isaac said . . . "When Hannah comes to you next Friday night, at the moment of passion, when you kiss her on the lips, let her breathe into your mouth. Then, you will be as one."

Isaac pulled up a plant, holding it aloft as if he were holding a severed head, a child's head, the roots with their clumps of earth looking like dangling veins and muscles.

"Spinach beet," Isaac said. "It's good for the bowels."

Isaac put the plant into his bag and walked on, leaving Moses, momentarily shivering, in the declining afternoon sun.

That Friday, in the middle of the night, Moses woke to find Hannah in his bed.

"Take me in your arms," she said.

Moses did.

"Come into me," she said.

With a shudder, Moses did.

"Kiss me on the lips," she said.

She was lovely as moonlight. And she drew Moses to her as the sun draws moisture from the fertile earth.

Moses bent his face toward hers.

"Kiss me," Hannah repeated.

Moses could smell her body, the tidal smell of the sea as it reaches farther and farther up the shore, sending rivulets around rocks, carving channels in the sand, undermining cliffs . . .

"Kiss me," Hannah breathed, urgently—as Moses hesitated.

His lips were so close to hers, he could feel her breath beginning to mingle with his.

"Why have you come to me?" he asked.

"Moses . . . ," she said, "kiss me!"

She moved her hips and drew her fingers along his shoulder blades as if she were coaxing the wings of a newly-hatched butterfly to unfold.

"Why are people dying?" Moses asked.

"Don't you love me?" Hannah said, her eyes filling with tears.

"I love you with all my heart, with all my might, and with all my soul," Moses said. "I love you blasphemously, as I should love the Lord of Hosts, Blessed Be He. Why are you coming to me?"

"First," she begged, "*kiss me.*"

Moses pulled back.

"Every other test your father gave me, happened before Sabbath," Moses said. "This test I must do *on* the Sabbath . . . Why?"

"You told me you loved me with all your heart, with all your soul, and with all your might," Hannah said.

"Blasphemously," Moses agreed, gazing into her eyes, which suddenly seemed opaque—dark as a new moon. Moses shivered. "Tell me why you came to me tonight."

"Moses . . . ," she began.

"Tell me," he said.

"Please . . . ," she said, rolling her eyes as if sinking into fever.

"Every time we are together," Moses said, "someone dies."

Like her father, Hannah answered, "*Goyim* die."

Moses waited.

In a dead voice, she explained:

"Each time we make love, you give more life to the Golem, which my father made from the bloody mud where Jews died in the pogrom. The Golem is our revenge. *God's* vengeance. Tonight, when we make love, when our breath mingles, the Golem will gain eternal life, the strength to destroy all the enemies of our people."

"So much blood?" Moses asked.

"No more than *they* have spilled," she said. "No more than was spilled to free Israel from Pharoah's bondage."

"And me?" Moses asked. "What will happen to me?"

"You will be the Saviour of the Jews," Hannah said.

Moses waited. He felt his strength ebbing, his eyes clouding.

"You and I shall spend eternity embraced," she said, again moving her hips, "as we are now."

"Eternity?" Moses said.

He could barely see her lips as they moved toward his.

"Together," she whispered . . . "We shall be together for always. As one . . ."

"A vampire," Moses gasped. "David was right!"

As he felt her lips touch his, Moses pushed her away with all his might.

From the darkness, he heard a sigh.

"If not you, who?" Hannah said. "If not now, when? Moses . . ."

Moses struggled out of the bed, gasping for breath.

"You don't understand," Hannah said. "Your children's children's children will face an enemy greater than Pharoah, greater than Ahasuerus . . . You can stop this."

Blindly, Moses rushed from the room.

"Their blood . . . ," the voice whispered. "Their blood is on your hands."

Outside, Moses stood under the Sabbath moon.

Gentile blood . . . Jewish blood . . . Either way his hands were stained.

Moses turned his face to God and asked, "Why? Why did you choose me?"

 *seven*

I

According to *The Zohar*, the Kabbalistic "Book of Splendor," in 1740—5500—"the gates of wisdom would open." And, throughout the gentile world, the gates of wisdom *were* opening—although not as *The Zohar* meant.

In Great Britain, David Hume published the third volume of his *Treatise of Human Nature*, "Of Morals." In France, the Comte de Buffon published his translation of Isaac Newton's *Fluxions*. In America, in Philadelphia, Benjamin Franklin was studying meteorology, the effect of the rotation of the earth on trans-Atlantic crossings, and a phenomenon introduced to him by the Scottish lecturer Dr. Archibald Spencer: electricity. And, in Prussia, Voltaire, fresh from experiments in physics, was extolling the benefits of the Enlightenment to his pupil, the recently-crowned king, Frederick the Great, who had just introduced in his domain freedom of the press and religion. In Plissa, twins—a boy and a girl—were born to the glass-maker, Heschel, called *Hodosh*, the Newcomer, and his wife Miriam, daughter of Shmu'el, the butcher.

According to my grandfather's brother—Heschel's namesake—Heschel the Newcomer was a big man, "like the giant Og," the Amorite, ruler of Bashan, who lost sixty towns to the tribe of Menasseh. And like Og—Heschel said—Heschel the Newcomer had a mysterious ancestry.

"My grandmother"—Heschel told me—"claimed he was the son of a fallen angel," one of the guardians who lusted after the daughters of man and, coupling with them, engendered monsters. "She said his father was the Angel of Anger."

When he was six years old, Heschel the Newcomer appeared in the center of town, alone, naked, on the night of a full moon.

Perhaps he'd strayed from some traveling couple. Or been abandoned. Or—as one story had it—walked over the mountains from the south, since, according to Heschel, he spoke Italian, although it's possible no one in Plissa ever had heard Italian. Maybe the *Italian* was some other foreign language that, in later generations, was identified as Italian because Heschel the Newcomer, as a young man, went to Genoa, where he learned the glassmaking trade.

Or maybe Heschel the Newcomer was the child of some Christian woman, who could not raise him for one reason or another. Her husband decided the boy was not his own. The family was too poor to feed him. Or too sick to raise him.

Or maybe Heschel the Newcomer *was* one of the *Nephilim*,

one of the children of the lascivious union of angels and humans.

At six—when he was found, laughing in the moonlight—Heschel the Newcomer was the size of a ten-year-old. At ten, he was as tall as a man. When he was fully grown, he was—according to my great-great-grandmother, according to Heschel—over seven feet tall.

"But graceful," Heschel said, "like an aristocrat."

Heschel the Newcomer was adopted by a childless couple: Isaac, who may or may not also have been a glassmaker and whose name may not have been Isaac, and Isaac's wife, whose name has been lost—dim figures, who, like faded shapes in an otherwise vivid fresco, are made harder to notice by the more brightly colored images around them.

Heschel the Newcomer. Heschel the Glassmaker. Heschel the Egyptian—which is what my grandfather called him.

When I asked why, my grandfather shook his head and went back to eating the corn flakes he had every night for supper after he came home from work. The big meal of the day was lunch. And it was during lunch the next day when, glancing at my grandfather, I asked my grandmother why my grandfather called Heschel the Newcomer "the Egyptian."

My grandmother shushed me. My grandfather ignored me.

After my grandfather had his nap and went back to the grocery store, my grandmother uncharacteristically raised the subject.

"Never, never again ask about him"—she meant Heschel the Newcomer.

When I pressed her to tell me why, she spit—a precaution against the evil eye—and whispered, "Because he was a *kuntsen macher*."

A magician.

A glassmaker. A magician . . .

When my grandmother first confided this secret to me, I assumed that the two crafts—glassmaking and magic— were separate. That Heschel the Newcomer was—I don't know—a glassmaker by day and a magician by night. It seemed an arbitrary combination.

But, while researching this book, I found that, in some traditions, making glass was associated with magic—a kind of alchemy that went back to Shinar, home of Terach, father of Abraham.

According to Samuel Kurinsky in *The Glassmakers: An Odyssey of the Jews, The First Three Thousand Years*, a piece of manufactured glass was "found at the ancient city of Eridu (Abu Sharein), sixteen miles southwest of Ur, in Shinar. . . . The date of the glass object was later fixed at between 2047–2039 B.C.E.," Kurinsky wrote. "Both the date and the location are those attributed to the tribe of Terach," Abraham's father, "prior to its move to Canaan."

Kurinsky notes "a symbiotic association between the wandering Jews and the art of glassmaking," a craft, Kurinsky writes, that, unlike other skills—potterymaking, metalsmithing, viticulture—"is unique among the arts in that it was invented only once in all human history; the knowledge of that process wound its way out into the world in ever-widening spirals with the people who developed it and passed their knowledge on to succeeding generations."

A secret process. Silica and an alkali, sand and potash, fused at high temperature, with lead for brilliance, metallic oxides for color, a practice essentially unchanged over the millennia, alchemy because it transforms one substance into another.

Because it can be used to penetrate mysteries, both mystical and rational.

Made into lenses—glass reveals *hidden* worlds. The macrocosm—with telescopes. The microcosm—with microscopes.

Made into mirrors—from Snow White's to Alice's Looking-glass—glass reveals *alternate* worlds.

Spinoza, the apostate Jewish philosopher, thought the mind was a lens through which one could understand God. Rationally. Logically.

Paracelsus, the alchemist, called the moon the *"speculum venenosum magnum naturae*, the great poisonous mirror of nature," which is infected by human gaze—especially by the gaze of a menstruating woman—and, in turn, infects those who gaze on it.

Lenses focus the beams of the sun and make fire.

Mirrors reflect reality.

Lenses reveal the mysteries of the atom and the stars.

Mirrors steal souls.

Lenses magnify.

Mirrors lie.

Lenses reduce.

Mirrors mimic.

Lenses tell the truth.

Mirrors distort.

Lenses distort.

Mirrors tell the truth—like the one at Nisanoff's, photographed by Edith Morgan, which displayed the secret, tense side of my paternal grandfather.

Mirrors and lenses.

The old world and the new. The Middle Ages and the Enlightenment.

II

Heschel the Newcomer's wife, Miriam, had freckles—according to a family tradition so strong that, when my grandfather's brother used to tease my first cousin, Aileen, about her freckles, he called her "another Miriam." And apparently Miriam had red hair—like the mysterious Hannah. Like Heschel.

Heschel . . . Hannah.

Red hair. Magic . . .

Maybe the stories of the two strangers—Hannah and Heschel—had a common root? Maybe only one red-haired stranger came to Plissa?

Maybe the stranger who seduced Moses was a male not a female, an incubus not a succubus? Maybe my seduced ancestor was a woman not a man? Maybe the seducer—demon or con artist—was Heschel not Hannah?

Red hair, freckles . . .

Not much to go on.

To imagine Miriam, I—like a mirror—have stolen Aileen's soul. Aileen's personality.

When Aileen and I were sixteen, everyone said we looked, not just like brother and sister, but like twins.

"Two peas in a pod," our grandmother said.

"Real *Hodoshes*," Heschel said.

My sister, Bea, who did not look like a Hodosh, was jealous.

"You and Aileen don't look anything alike," she said.

That summer, Aileen's parents sent her to Providence to spend some time with our grandparents, to visit Pembroke College, which had not yet succumbed to institutional androgyny and become one with Brown. She was all legs and elbows.

And sarcasm.

When we necked in my grandparents' cellar—which still had an old-fashioned 1930s washing machine with a mangle—when I slipped my hand under her dress and touched the moist cotton between her legs, she said, "Don't start something you can't finish."

Did that mean she wanted me to make love to her? Or that she wanted me to stop?

I stopped.

Tilting her head with a teenage girl's wry superiority, she said, "See what you missed?"

And, shrugging off the thin straps holding up her sundress, she exposed her naked chest.

The fact that she wasn't wearing a bra—this was in 1961—was as shocking, maybe more shocking, than her exhibitionism.

Watching me, as I gazed at her freckled breast—"another Miriam"—Aileen covered herself. And smiled.

I imagine Miriam smiling like that—as Heschel the

Newcomer, braver than I was—embraced her, secretly, shamefully, ecstatically between their betrothal, *kiddushin*, and their marriage, *nissu'in*, that embrace an offense against both God and men.

But Heschel the Newcomer—or Heschel the Newcomer as I imagine him—stood arms akimbo, head thrown back, laughingly, rebelliously challenging both man and God.

"Jews don't bow down," my father used to say, expressing his own peculiar description of a fundamental principle of Judaism, "not to men, not to kings, not to idols, not to God Himself."

My father, Heschel the Newcomer, Abraham . . .

I grew up seeing the three of them like characters in a 1930s popular front mural of heroic Americans, in profile, all facing the future.

Washington, Lincoln, FDR.

Soldiers at Bunker Hill, Gettysburg, Normandy.

A farmer holding a pitchfork, a tradesman in an apron, a laborer with a wrench.

My father, Heschel the Newcomer, Abraham.

All, heads up, eyes clear, resolute. All, arguing with God. My father turning the religious debate with the Almighty into a union negotiation for a new contract. Abraham, too, negotiating a new contract: the Covenant. "I am El Shaddai," the Lord God said to Abraham when Abraham was ninety-nine years old; "walk before me and be perfect."

But Abraham—and the other Old Testament Patriarchs—were *not* perfect. They were cranky, contentious, obstinate, fanatical, opinionated, uncompromising, contrary . . .

". . . intractable, implacable, irresponsible," Heschel said, describing Heschel the Newcomer, "defiant, cocksure, and proud."

Heschel the Newcomer was forever questioning the old laws.

Why this? Why that? *Why?*

Like a rabbi niggling over a Talmudic text.

Why should a man be exempt from reciting the Shema because of anxiety?

Abaye says that reciting the *Shema* requires intention—enough awareness to make the prayer meaningful, awareness that may be checked by anxiety.

Rava disagrees. The world is so full of anxiety—he says—that if anxiety were enough to relieve someone from the obligation of reciting the *Shema*, no one would ever pray.

What were Abraham's ten trials? Rashi and Rambam do not agree.

Why?

When sages disagree—as Hillel and Shammai did during the Talmudic period, as the Mitnaggedim and the Hasidim did centuries later—how can one know which side reflects God's will?

Why isn't God's will obvious?

Or a better example, given Heschel the Newcomer's origins: *Why must a Jewish community concern itself with an abandoned child?*

An abandoned child—alone, laughing in the moonlight—can only be trouble!

Why was it abandoned?

It's a bastard . . . It's a goy . . . It's a goyish bastard . . .

It's someone's shame.

Why must it become *our* shame?

Our problem?

If an abandoned child is found in a city with a mixed population, both Jews and non-Jews, should the child be considered a Jew or a non-Jew?

Rav says, If most of the city's residents are non-Jews, the child is considered a non-Jew.

Shmuel says, If most of the city's residents are Jews, the child is considered a Jew.

But what if the residents are equally divided among Jews and non-Jews?

Rav and Shmuel say the child is considered a Jew.

By lineage.

But Jew or non-Jew, the abandoned child—Rambam says—must be considered a ward of the Jewish community, which must feed, clothe, house, and otherwise support the child.

Rabbi Abba bar Zavda says . . .

Rav Yosef, Rabbi Elazar, Rabbi Gamliel . . .

This rabbi says . . . That rabbi says . . .

God says . . . Abraham says . . .

God: *Because the outcry of Sodom and Amorrah has become great, and because their sin has been very grave, I will descend and see: If they act in accordance with its outcry— then destruction!*

Abraham: *Will you . . . stamp out the righteous along with the wicked? What if there should be fifty righteous people in the city . . . ?*

God: *If I find in Sodom fifty righteous people in the midst of the city, then I would spare the entire place on their account.*

Q. *What if the fifty righteous people should lack five?*

A. *I will not destroy if I find there forty-five.*

Q. *What if forty would be found there?*

A. *I will not act on account of the forty.*

Q. *What if thirty be found there?*

A. *I will not act if I find there thirty.*

Q. *What if twenty be found there?*

A. *I will not destroy on account of the twenty.*

Q. *What if ten would be found there?*

A. *I will not destroy on account of the ten.*

Abraham's haggling with God seemed—when I was a child—mankind's proudest moment.

Man questioning God's will.

A human protest against *the way things are!*

Why kill the righteous along with the wicked?

Why kill the wicked?

Why death? Why pain? Why suffering?

Why are children abandoned?

Why are girls raped?

Why pogroms?

Why the Holocaust?

If God could have made any world possible or impossible, why make a world crazed with conflict?

Why . . . Why . . .

Like children, the Sages' wisdom can be reduced to that one word.

Why?

Why? The question my father's life asked the world: *Why is there injustice?*

Why? The question I ask of my mother's life: *Why did she go crazy?*

III

In Plissa, marriage was a delicately balanced construction—a kind of mobile made out of money, education, and *yichus*, status. Arranging a marriage involved complex engineering.

In *Life Is With People*, Mark Zborowski and Elizabeth Herzog repeat the Talmudic anecdote about a gentile who once asked a Jew, "If your God created the world in only six days, what's He been doing since?"

"Arranging marriages," said the Jew.

"That's all?" said the gentile.

"If you think it's so easy," said the Jew, *"you* try it."

The gentile—an aristocratic Roman matron—gathered two thousand slaves, a thousand male and a thousand female, and within a matter of hours had paired them off.

The next morning, she came upon the first pair in the marketplace.

The man had a black eye. The woman, a scowl.

"What happened?" the gentile asked the couple.

"He's a fool," the woman said.

"She's a shrew," the man said.

A little farther on, she came upon the second couple, bickering.

Near them was the third couple, who were pelting each other with fruit and vegetables.

Not one of the thousand couples got along.

The gentile went back to the Jew and said:

"There is no god like your God, blessed be He . . ."

IV

Miriam's family was poor. Heschel the Newcomer's adopted parents were comfortable. Heschel's prospects were promising. Glassmaking was a good trade. It was a sensible alliance.

And Heschel the Newcomer and Miriam loved each other.

Everyone in the village congratulated the *shadkhen*, the matchmaker.

To ensure a sweet life, the night before the wedding ceremony, Miriam's hair was braided with sugar, which stuck to her scalp when her hair was cut, making her cry out.

Hi-va and *Hi-ya*—shouts of pain—were also the names of the sons of the fallen angels and their mortal wives.

Shouts followed by tears, as Miriam wept for her lost hair, her lost maidenhood . . . Tears followed by resignation, as the old women clipped and burned Miriam's fingernails and toenails . . . Resignation followed by joy at the prospect of the pleasures she and her future husband would share . . . All the pleasures, including the pleasures of the marriage bed, which, as the *Zohar* says, "a man should be as zealous to enjoy . . . as . . . the Sabbath."

Miriam's *sheytl* was imported from Berlin, a wig so realistic, so beautiful, it seemed to defeat the purpose of shaving her head—which was to avoid attracting the *goyim*.

And Miriam did attract the *goyim*, especially the officers from the local regiment who would make admiring comments to her—just as officers would a century and a quarter later to my grandmother and her sister, Bella and Ruth.

How many Heschels? How many Moseses? How many Davids in my family? How many gentile officers casting lustful looks at Jewesses? Names, characteristics, themes are repeated over the years, until my family's history begins to seem like a sonata.

Or—a more homely trope—like the kind of wallpaper that decorated the attic room I slept in as a teenager, on which a rustic couple—Jack and Jill? Hansel and Gretel? Moses and Hannah? Heschel the Newcomer and Miriam? their children, the twins?—walked in a wood, indicated by a single, repeating weeping willow.

V

After the wedding, Heschel the Newcomer and Miriam traveled to Genoa—for reasons that have been lost.

Maybe Heschel the Newcomer had family there? Maybe Heschel the Newcomer wanted to introduce his new wife to glassmaking colleagues? To friends?

Once on the road, Heschel the Newcomer and Miriam pretended that they were brother and sister. To forestall the *goyim* from killing Heschel the Newcomer to get Miriam.

Just like Abraham and Sarah in Pharoah's court.

Just like Abraham and Sarah in Abimalech's court.

The themes in my family's history have deep roots.

Abraham's wife, Sarah, was as beautiful—more beautiful—than the first woman, Eve.

And, when, to escape a famine in Canaan, Abraham went to Egypt, he—according to *Genesis*—told Sarah, "When the Egyptians see you, they will say, 'This is his wife!'; then, they will kill me, but you they will let live. Please say that you are my sister, that it may go well with me for your sake, and that I may live on account of you."

That it may go well with me for your sake.

According to the commentary in *The Stone Edition* of *The Chumash*, edited by Rabbi Nosson Scherman, "The sense of Abraham's statement was that if the nobles of Egypt were to shower him with gifts to win his 'sister's' hand, the masses would be afraid to harm him, and Sarah's safety would be assured. But his plan did not succeed, for Sarah's exceptional beauty brought about a different turn of events."

Sarah was taken to Pharaoh to be his wife.

"And he"—Pharaoh—"treated Abram well for her sake," continues *Genesis*, and Abraham "acquired sheep, cattle, donkeys, slaves and maidservants, female donkeys, and camels."

"Abraham pimped his wife," my grandfather's brother, Heschel, said—his own very un-Rabbinic commentary.

"Heschel!" my mother said, shocked.

"Abraham hid Sarah in a casket to protect her from the Egyptians," my father corrected Heschel, adding for Bea's and my benefit, "Those Egyptians had a reputation for being—"

"Horny," Heschel interrupted.

"Sensual," my father said. "But the tax collectors found her and—"

"Abraham ran the same scam twice," Heschel said.

After Egypt, when Abraham went to Gerar, the land of the Philistines—for the same reason: famine—Abraham again passed Sarah off as his sister.

For the same reasons.

With the same effect.

In Gerar, "Abraham did not ask Sarah's permission to use this ruse," according to the *Stone* commentary, "because she would have refused due to her previous abduction by Pharaoh. On the other hand, he did not expect an abduction to take place . . ."

But, like Pharaoh, Abimalech, the king of Gerar, took Sarah—either because "her beauty was so great at the age of ninety," according to the *Stone* commentary. Or because "he wished to marry into the august family of Abraham."

In Egypt, in Gerar, why didn't Abraham immediately explain that Sarah was his wife?

Why did he continue to lie? Heschel wanted to know.

"He didn't lie," said my father.

Sometimes it's important to shade the truth a little . . . , my father had said as he changed the prices in the books we'd bought at Johnson's Bookstore.

Shaded truth.

"Abraham didn't lie?" Heschel asked. "What would *you* call it?"

"The honesty of the Patriarchs makes it impossible to

believe that Abraham would have told an outright lie . . . ," the *Stone* commentaries explain. A "man often refers to his relative as his sister . . ."

That was no lady that was my sister . . .

Shaded truth.

"Abram actually never told Sarai to say that she was single," according to Rabbi Aryeh Kaplan's translation of the Ladino classic, *MeAm Lo'ez*, which was first published a few years before Heschel the Newcomer and Miriam set out for Genoa. "But he did not want" the Egyptians "to know that she was *his* wife . . ."

More trimming.

"Abram wept all night," Robert Graves and Raphael Patai wrote in *Hebrew Myths*, "praying that Sarai would keep her virginity."

She did—with the help of an angelic bodyguard who whacked Pharaoh with a stick every time Pharaoh touched so much as Sarah's slipper.

For taking Sarah, both Pharaoh and Abimalech were punished with *Ra'athan*, a skin disease, possibly syphilis according to the *MeAm Lo'ez*, leprosy according to Louis Ginzberg's *The Legends of the Jews*.

And, in both courts, until Sarah was restored to Abraham, all women were stopped—painfully—from delivering their babies, even those who had already breached.

"Of course . . . you were correct," Pharaoh told Abraham, according to the *MeAm Lo'ez*. "The Egyptians are indeed shameless . . . But why could you not tell me the truth privately? I would have returned her to you immediately."

To God, Abimalech—who could still see the fires of

Sodom burning in the distance—said, "When I heard about the Great Flood and the punishment meted out to the builders of the Tower of Babel, I wondered how all could have been punished."

This is also from the *MeAm Lo'ez*.

"Were there no good men among them?" Abimalech asked God. "Now, since I am being punished for nothing, the question bothers me again . . . Didn't" Abraham "say to me, 'She is my sister'?"

"Is it Your practice to destroy nations without cause?" Abimalech asked God, according to the *Stone* commentary.

"You should have waited a few days and taken time to investigate the matter more thoroughly," God told Abimalech, according to the *MeAm Lo'ez*. "You should not have rushed so much."

"But how will" Abraham "believe that I have not touched her?" Abimalech asked, according to Rabbi Moshe Wissman's *The Midrash Says*.

Abraham "is a prophet," God told Abimalech. "Ask him to forgive you . . . or else you will die."

Abraham not only forgave Abimalech, he prayed for him, which—according to Rabbi William Braude's translation of the *Pesikta Rabbati*—"shows that a man's compassion for his fellows will be followed by God's compassion for him . . ."

Rabbi Braude performed my father and mother's wedding ceremony—at my grandparents' house on Congress Avenue in Providence.

The wedding did not take place in a synagogue. Because my father had rejected the faith of his fathers? Or because my mother was already pregnant?

Given my father's atheism, why didn't my mother and father get married in a civil ceremony?

If my mother was pregnant, why did a rabbi agree to officiate?

And why was Larry Ascot present?

Why . . .

Faye, my mother's sister, claims that, when my mother and father first met at the Jug End, the roadhouse between Boston and Providence, she introduced her lover Larry Ascot to my father as her brother . . .

Heschel and Binzy claim that my father knew he was dating a gangster's girlfriend. And—for the risk of it, for the fun of it—took my mother to a nearby motel, where, signing in, he claimed my mother was his sister . . .

The past is a hall of mirrors.

According to Irving M. Bunim's commentary on *Pirke Avoth, Ethics From Sinai,* Sarah's abductions by Pharaoh and Abimalech were two of the ten *nisyonoth* or trials God sent Abraham to see if he would "turn in defiance and rebellion, or at least question his Maker in asperity about His justice."

But, Bunim points out, "not once did" Abraham "complain or grow bitter."

In fact, by the time Abraham reached Gerar, he was nonchalant enough to make love to Sarah in a spot where Abimalech could see them.

Just like my father—leaving his car in front of the motel where Larry Ascot could see it . . .

Just like Binzy dancing with my mother in front of my father as he played the *Hong Kong Blues* on his cornet . . .

Stop the music!

VI

"Funny to hear *you* defending the Bible," Heschel said to my father, as they argued about Abraham's motives.

"Funny to hear *you* attacking it," my father said.

Unlike his brother—my grandfather—Heschel had assimilated. He smoked cigarettes—Old Golds—and drank whiskey—Canadian Club—not *schnapps*, beer not sweet wine. He read the *Providence Journal* not the *Forward*.

And, although Heschel was faithful while his wife was alive, after she died, he developed a reputation as a Casanova.

Heschel was always telling off-color jokes, pointing out attractive women, and commenting on the progress of his younger relatives' puberty or his own generation's climacteric.

"Your sister," Heschel would say to me at the beach, "she's beginning to look good in a bathing suit."

Or, at dinner, when his sister Pearl would fiddle with the high collar of her dress, he'd announce, "Someone open a window. Poor Pearl's having a hot flash."

Heschel pointed out that Abraham and Sarah's furtive and passionate coupling in Abimalech's court was when Abraham was 100 and Sarah was ninety.

"Jews come from good stock," said Heschel, who had just turned seventy and bragged that *he* showed no signs of flagging potency.

VII

Despite his assimilation, Heschel was observant—unlike my grandfather, who, despite his tendency to cling to the old ways, was not.

Heschel went to *schul*. Heschel, at least while his wife was alive, kept kosher—even worrying, like a Talmudist, over points of dietary law like: *Are false teeth part of the body or appliances.*

If false teeth were part of the body, one needed only one pair.

If false teeth were appliances—like spoons and forks— one needed separate sets for dairy and meat.

Heschel tried to draw my grandfather into arguments about religion and politics. Unsuccessfully. So, usually, Heschel would turn his guns on my father, by whose socialism and atheism Heschel pretended to be appalled.

"So," my father asked Heschel, "how come all of a sudden you've switched sides?"

"I didn't say Abraham was *wrong* to trick Pharaoh . . . To trick Abimalech . . . ," Heschel said. "It was part of God's plan."

Heschel was sullen.

"And Isaac?" my father asked.

Isaac played the same trick on Abimalech that Abraham had, passing off *his* wife, Rebekah, as *his* sister; revealing the scam only after Abimalech had taken Rebekah into his palace; and being paid off as his father, Abraham, had been—with land by the guilty, but not yet adulterous, king.

Paid off by Abimalech twice.

To *get* Rebekah *before* he knew that Rebekah was married. To get *rid* of Rebekah *after* he knew that Rebekah was married.

"And Isaac?" my father repeated.

Heschel shrugged. And, glancing at me, implying something that to this day escapes me, Heschel said, "Like father, like son . . ."

Heschel's argument with my father seemed to be not about Abraham's behavior, but about my father's—the result of some undercurrent of resentment that found an echo in the Biblical stories. Some undercurrent of resentment that connected my father to Abraham in a way that I will probably never discover.

"Maybe because your father made a new covenant"— his own covenant—"with God," my ex-wife suggested.

She had an appreciation of religious nuances—*Jewish* nuances—that I lacked. That only someone raised outside the faith could have understood.

Just as Abraham and Sarah changed *their* names once they made their covenant with God—from *Abram* and *Sarai*, my father changed *his* name—from *Zvi Aaron* to *Abe, Abraham*—once *he* renegotiated *his* covenant with God. A covenant that did not establish faith but broke it.

My father chose to believe not in God but in Man.

"An atheist like you . . . ," Heschel said to my father, shrugging. "What do you care about Isaac, about Abraham . . . ? An iconoclast like you . . ."

An iconoclast like Abraham, my father's namesake—who shattered *his* father's gods . . .

An iconoclast like Heschel the Newcomer, who, as a young man, once disrupted the Sabbath by storming through Plissa, ranting, shouting that the townsfolk prayed to God, but worshipped riches.

What outraged Heschel the Newcomer—what act of hypocrisy or greed—is lost and, like an unseen planet exerting some visible pull, can only be surmised by its effects.

"Revolutionists run in the family," my father said.

VIII

Heschel the Newcomer and Miriam traveled to Genoa in "Veadar," the intercalary month between Adar (February–March) and Nisan (March–April), the chronological equivalent in the Gregorian calendar of a hidden room.

They traveled by coach. A few days before they reached Genoa, they stopped overnight at an inn.

The single large room had a hard-packed dirt floor. It reeked of human sweat, damp ashes, beets, potatoes, roots, buried things. Overhead, the beams were charred, evidence of an old fire. On the central table, meat steamed in a wooden platter. The innkeeper's beard glistened with grease. On the sand-covered floor, in the corner, its legs bound with straw, lay a lamb with large pleading eyes.

At the inn, Heschel the Newcomer and Miriam met an English architect named Bird.

One family tradition claims that the *Bird* was a *Wren*—

Sir Christopher—who helped rebuild London after the Great Fire of 1666. But Wren died in 1723.

Over supper, Bird drew Heschel the Newcomer into a discussion about the nature of the soul.

Heschel the Newcomer quoted the *Zohar*, explaining that, just as Noah had three sons, the soul had three parts: the *Neshamah* or supersoul, the *ruah* or spirit, and the *nefesh* or vital soul—a belief that, Janus-like, looks backward to Egyptian mythology—with its *Ba, Ka,* and *ib*; soul, spirit, and heart—and forward to Freud's *Ego, Superego,* and *Id*.

Taking his cue from Descartes, Bird imagined the soul like wheat that could be winnowed from the chaff of the body.

Bird was a Freemason and a Deist, who believed in the fellowship of all men, whatever their religion or origins.

He pressed food on Heschel the Newcomer and Miriam, who politely declined and ate the Kosher meal they had brought.

He poured Heschel the Newcomer glasses of wine, which Heschel the Newcomer didn't touch . . . Which Bird drank. Along with his own.

Bird asked Heschel the Newcomer his views on Spinoza.

Heschel the Newcomer had never heard of Spinoza.

Bird was surprised.

"Surely, you know Spinoza, sir," Bird said to Heschel the Newcomer. "He is a Jew."

Bird liked Jews. Through his Masonic lodge, he knew about the Kabbalah, which he had read in a French abridgment. He liked a taint of Jewish mysticism, a hint of Templar magic, to give his rationalism an oriental spice. He imagined himself a Crusader, fighting not Saracens, but ignorance.

The fire cast spidery Giacometti shadows up the wall and across the ceiling. Bird pounded the wooden table and declaimed Alexander Pope's recently published *Universal Prayer*:

Father of all! in every age,
In every clime adored,
By saint, by savage, and by sage,
Jehovah, Jove, or Lord!

"*I am the Lord, thy God,*" Heschel the Newcomer quoted. "*Thou shalt have no other gods before Me.*"

"All deities, sir, are merely man's aspirations to the good," Bird said.

"*Shema Yisroel,*" Heschel the Newcomer said, "*Adonai Elohenu, Adonai Echod.*"

"*Unless these differences can be resolved,*" Bird said, quoting Cicero, "*mankind will continue to live in the grossest error . . .*"

"*Hear, O Israel,*" Heschel the Newcomer repeated in Italian, "*The Lord our God, the Lord is One.*"

"Stubborn," Bird said.

"Heathen," Heschel the Newcomer said.

"Mule," Bird said.

"Better a mule," Heschel the Newcomer said, "than an ass."

"Why, sir, do you insist on this eccentric and singular attitude?" Bird said. "Why will you not join the common humanity?"

"*It is not because you are the most numerous of peoples that the Lord set His heart on you and chose you,*" Heschel the Newcomer quoted from *Deuteronomy*. "*Indeed, you are the smallest of peoples; but it was because the Lord loved you.*"

"So, sir, like the followers of John Calvin," Bird said, "you consider yourself one of the elect?"

"We have the burden and joy of observing the laws of the Lord, our God, Blessed be He," Heschel the Newcomer said.

"How do you know?" my daughter asked when she read this chapter.

"How do I know that Heschel the Newcomer considered himself chosen?" I said.

"*. . . the fire cast spidery Giacometti shadows,*" she quoted, "*up the wall and across the ceiling.* How do you know that's what the fire did?"

"*Before 1800, there are fewer and fewer facts,*" I quoted, defending myself. "*I have to follow clues to my family history like Hansel following bread crumbs out of the forest.*"

"If you're Hansel," my daughter asked, "who's Gretel?"

IX

"Your sister is beautiful," Bird told Heschel.

Heschel was silent.

Bird took out a gold necklace and draped it around Miriam's neck.

When Heschel objected, Bird angrily said, "Why deny your sister such luxury?"

"I can't accept it," Miriam said, taking off the necklace and giving it back to Bird. "I'm frail. The gold is too heavy."

Just before dawn, Heschel the Newcomer was awakened by a chill. The air smelled bad, like burning skin, like burned fingernails.

Heschel the Newcomer sat up and, disoriented, glanced around at the bodies, which lay on benches, on the floor like corpses. A wick sizzled in an oil lamp, made out of a clay shard that looked like a child's severed ear.

Miriam was gone.

So was Bird.

Where Miriam had slept was the gold necklace.

Outside, Heschel the Newcomer ran first one way, then another along the road. The forest, lit by rotting phosphorescent logs, looked like Gehenna.

Heschel the Newcomer fell to his knees and wept.

When Heschel—my grandfather's brother—used to tell the story to Bea and me, when we were kids, when he came to this part, he described how a crow looked up from where it was feeding on dried dung and asked Heschel the Newcomer what was the matter.

"Did he really talk to a crow?" asked my son, who like my daughter wants to sift the story, separating out the wheat from the chaff, the soul of the tale from the mere circumstances.

I don't know.

If Bird could have been a Wren, maybe he also could have been a *crow*.

Maybe Bird left a message for Heschel the Newcomer,

and over the years the message became words in the crow's beak.

Maybe Heschel the Newcomer was so distraught he thought the crow spoke to him.

Maybe the crow really *did* speak to him.

I don't know.

"Yes," I told my son, who is six years old. "Heschel the Newcomer really talked to a crow."

Q. How do you know?

A. It's part of the story. My grandfather's brother told me.

Q. Where did he learn it?

A. His grandmother told him.

And I'm telling you and your sister, and you'll tell it to your grandchildren, and they'll tell it to their grandchildren, and, as long as the story is told, Heschel the Newcomer will be searching for Miriam.

X

The crow says to Heschel the Newcomer, "So why the long face? That's what the waiter said to the horse when it sat down at Lindy's . . ."

Rimshot.

"I wanna tell you," said the crow. "I just flew in from the Coast. And, boy, are my wings tired."

Rimshot.

"What is this?" said the crow. "What kind of an audience are you? You think *you* got trouble. Let me tell you about *my* trouble. I go home, find my wife in the nest with my best friend. I'm shocked. I say to my friend, *I have to, but you . . . !"*

Rimshot.

"So," said the crow, "Abraham goes to Pharaoh, and Pharoah says, *Women . . . They're all the same. They lie, they cheat . . .*

"Abraham says, *Some women are faithful.*

"Pharaoh says, *Some women! Some? Have you ever met a woman who was faithful?"*

"Nodding, Abraham says, *Take my wife."*

Please!

So Pharaoh did.

Rimshot!

XI

Following the crow's directions, Heschel the Newcomer caught up with Bird and Miriam—where or when is not clear. Possibly near a town in the Tyrol called Arnbach.

Trembling with rage and exhaustion, Heschel the Newcomer accused Bird of abducting his wife.

"But what do you expect," Bird said, "when you pretend she is your sister?"

Gently, almost lovingly, Heschel the Newcomer held Bird's face between his hands, each one of which was as large as Bird's head. With a twist, Heschel the Newcomer could have broken Bird's neck.

Miriam had traveled with Bird for three days. How could Heschel the Newcomer be sure she had not been violated?

"Ask her," Bird said, outraged at the suggestion he would force himself on Miriam. "Don't you trust your own wife to tell you the truth?"

Heschel the Newcomer stole a glance at Miriam, whose face was aflame with humiliation. He asked and Miriam assured him that Bird had treated her with every courtesy.

Heschel the Newcomer took two slips of paper.

According to the old custom, Heschel the Newcomer said, he would leave one slip blank. On the other slip, Heschel the Newcomer said, he would write the word *guilty*.

He would put both slips into a box.

With God guiding her hand, Miriam would pick one.

If she picked the blank slip, it would be proof of her innocence—and, Heschel the Newcomer said, Bird would go on his way, a free man.

If she picked the slip that said *guilty*, it would be proof of her guilt—and, Heschel the Newcomer said, he would kill Bird on the spot.

With his back to them, Heschel the Newcomer wrote. Turning, he put the slips into the box—which he held out to Miriam.

Pick one, Heschel the Newcomer told Miriam.

Despite his iconoclasm, Heschel the Newcomer, with *shtetl* courtesy, usually averted his eyes in the presence of women, including his wife.

Now, however, he looked Miriam straight in the face.

Miriam understood—and smiled.

They both knew the old story, a favorite, about the Jew on trial for the ritual murder of a Christian child.

The Jew was innocent. But the court was rigged.

To preserve the illusion of fairness, the judge—according to tradition—took two slips of paper. Just as Heschel the Newcomer had.

One slip—the judge said—he would leave blank. Just as Heschel the Newcomer said he had.

On the other—the judge said—he would write the word *guilty*. Just as Heschel the Newcomer said he had.

The Jew would draw one of the two slips from a box, his hand guided by God. Just as Miriam would.

If the Jew drew the blank slip, he would go free. If the Jew drew the slip with the *guilty* verdict, he would die.

But, convinced of the Jew's guilt, the devious judge secretly wrote *guilty* on both slips. Just as Heschel the Newcomer had.

Suspecting treachery, the Jew drew out one slip—and ate it.

"How will we now determine your guilt?" the judge asked.

"Easy," the Jew said, "examine the slip left in the box."

Which the judge did.

Of course, the slip said *guilty*—which, as the Jew pointed out, meant the slip he had swallowed was blank.

By the judge's own rules, the Jew had been proved innocent.

The judge could not argue the Jew's claim without revealing his own dishonesty.

So the Jew was freed.

Miriam reached into the box and drew out a slip—which she ate.

XII

Long after Heschel the Newcomer and Miriam returned to Plissa, they remained childless.

Like Abraham and Sarah.

And, like Abraham and Sarah, they filled their days with good deeds—helping the poor and the sick, widows and abandoned children.

But the good deeds did not change their luck.

The Angel of Night refused to bless their seed.

Miriam's family blamed her childless state on Heschel the Newcomer, who—an *oyfgekummener*, an upstart, an orphan, probably a bastard—lived, they believed, under a curse.

According to one tradition, the curse had something to do with Heschel the Newcomer's origins—a malediction passed down from Heschel the Newcomer's father and his father's father.

According to another tradition, Heschel the Newcomer's curse was the result of impiety.

I'd imagined Heschel embracing his wife before his wedding.

Why?

In my original notes I wrote under "Heschel": *kisses on impure days.*

Beneath that I wrote—when? at least fifteen years ago—*patchwork shirt, Reuben, Heschel.*

When I was eight, my mother bought me a shirt made up of different colored squares—an "Ivy League" shirt she called it. I wore it on a visit to Providence. My grandfather called it my "coat of many colors."

That night, uncharacteristically, he came into the den where I slept in a trundle bed and told me about Joseph and his brothers, a story I'm sure I'd heard before.

But, whenever I think of the story of Joseph, I see my grandfather looming over the bed like some nightmare figure out of Goya, I smell the sweet raw reek of his butcher shop, I hear his voice, soft as the rumble of distant thunder, like the voice of God from the top of Sinai.

And what I remember most vividly about what he told me that night was how Reuben slept with his father's concubine, Bilhah.

"Of all the sins," my grandfather said, "lust is the one we must forgive the most."

Patchwork shirt, Reuben, Heschel.

Lust is the sin we must forgive the most.

Maybe my grandfather told me something about Heschel, something I've forgotten, something which explains my impression of Heschel as passionate enough to embrace his wife before they were married or while she was having her period—on an impure day.

A third tradition claims Heschel the Newcomer was cursed because of some act of anger.

Miriam had a miracle rabbi pray over her womb. On her way home from the ritual baths, she made sure to avoid dogs. She collected amulets and charms, slept with the full moon shining through the window onto her belly, made sure their bed was pointed north, and always kept near her a hard-boiled egg in a cloth bag with a piece of parchment on which a *tzaddik*, a holy man, had inscribed the letter *ches*, which, equaling the number eight, stood for Isaac, the child of Sarah's old age, the first Jewish child to be circumcised on the eighth day after his birth . . .

Ten barren years passed.

The rabbi told Heschel the Newcomer it was time to divorce Miriam.

Heschel the Newcomer refused. He loved his wife.

Heschel the Newcomer stormed into the prayer house and demanded an explanation from God.

Had he been negligent in his duties? Like Job, was he being tested? Why had *Hashem* denied them children?

Why?

Heschel the Newcomer shouted. He beat his breast. He argued. He negotiated.

He would give away half his fortune as a dowry for the one-eyed orphan, Fruma . . . He would rebuild the *schul* . . . He would do anything . . . if *Hashem* would just give him a child.

By chance, an itinerant Jew, a peddler, entered the prayer house as Heschel the Newcomer was ranting.

"A child?" the peddler asked.

"A son," Heschel said, already haggling.

"And," the peddler said, "if *Hashem* granted you a daughter . . . ?"

The peddler was filthy. His caftan was stained. The spots looked vaguely geographical—Spain on his left sleeve, Africa on his back, India over one hip—as if the cloth had been made from an old map. For a girdle, he used a piece of dirty rope, frayed at the ends like *payess*. His beard was matted, tangled with twigs. The pupils of his eyes were round and red like currants. His fingers were as thin as chicken bones. And, inside his rags, his limbs jiggled loose-jointed like a skeleton. His face was so covered with red, blue, and purple carbuncles, it looked as if his cheeks, forehead, and chin were studded with gems. He lifted up the hem of his caftan and blew his nose.

"Who are you?" Heschel the Newcomer asked.

"A peddler," the stranger said.

Heschel the Newcomer knew the tales of angels who appeared in the guise of vagabonds. Sunset would usher in Passover, the same day, 15 Nisan—March 29—an angel told Abraham Isaac would be born.

The peddler—Heschel the Newcomer decided—was Gabriel, the Angel God had sent to tell Sarah she would give birth at last.

Heschel the Newcomer grabbed the peddler, who, despite his frailty, struggled. They fell to the floor of the prayer house, as the scandalized men of Plissa dithered around them, crying out, but afraid to intervene.

"Let me go," the peddler said, echoing the Angel Jacob had wrestled millennia before at the ford of the Jabbok.

"I will not let thee go, except thou bless me," Heschel the Newcomer said—like the peddler, falling into the ancient formula.

"Meshuggener!" the peddler said.

"Give me a son!" Heschel the Newcomer demanded.

"Get off me," the peddler said, crushed under Heschel's weight.

"*Give me a son!*" Heschel the Newcomer shouted.

The peddler nodded.

Heschel the Newcomer released him.

The peddler lay, his chest heaving, as Heschel the Newcomer loomed over him.

"Whatever power I have to grant your wish . . . ," the peddler said. "May your seed be fruitful and multiply."

He sat up, adding:

"And may God forgive your violence toward a poor stranger."

That night, Heschel the Newcomer dreamed that from Miriam's belly grew a vine, green as a grass snake, which blindly felt its way along the bed to the wall, up the wall, and slipped through a crack in the roof—growing, probing insistently, like the middle finger of an ardent boy insinuating itself between his lover's legs.

Down the vine climbed, slid, slipped, tumbled, one after another, babies, hundreds of babies, male and female, blue-eyed and brown, plump and pink, the soles of the tiny feet creased like old leather.

The next harvest, Miriam gave birth to the twins, Yussel and Raizel—Joseph and Rose.

XIII

Heschel the Newcomer indulged Joseph and Rose, letting them run wild.

When Rose wove a crown of flowers as she had seen the gentile girls do, Heschel the Newcomer chided but did not punish her.

And he did not object when Joseph wandered aimlessly about Plissa, among Jew and gentile, watching, listening, pushing chest-high through flocks of sheep, dodging the hoofs of donkeys and the wheels of carts.

Yungatsh, a street urchin, Miriam's family called Joseph. Like the son of *prosteh yidn*, Jewish peasants.

Once when he was seven, Joseph was prowling through the market during the harvest fair. Jew and gentile had put up booths and were selling, trading, buying trinkets and essentials.

Hundreds of feet had churned the street into mud. Red, yellow, blue, and green ribbons fluttered from a pole. In the sunlight, amber beads glowed like embers. The spicy smell of gingerbread soldiers mingled with the spicier smell from the tanner in the next booth, where a man with a milky eye sold harnesses, boots, and saddles, which he had slung over some barrels, ready for invisible riders.

Joseph, shouldering his way between the wide hips of farm women and the high-booted legs of soldiers, wiggled to the front of every crowd, eager to see everything.

Everything . . .

Lace as delicate as the net of the first frost. Walnuts, which, with their ridges and neatly divided halves, looked like the withered brains of fairies. Dried fish metallically glistening. Rabbits hanging upside down, their back legs crossed. Cock pheasants with their red masks and yellow beaks.

In her lap, a woman held a half-plucked chicken, the naked skin covered in white bumps. Across from her a tinker tapped a sheet of tin, which from the back looked as bumpy as the chicken's skin.

A sheep's head mottled red and white, skull-like without its ears, and whatever was left of its lips primly pursed.

Muscular-looking cow tongues, arched and gray as ash, lined up in a row. Slabs of blue-veined cheese. Jams yellow as molten gold. Waxy combs, tessellated like a mosaic, dripping with honey. Sausages fat as baby arms. Dried peas like baby teeth.

In a gaily painted theater, one puppet threatened another puppet with a stick. Another booth sold silvery stars that spun, sending off sparks—of sunlight? of sulfur?—like firebirds.

Joseph strolled through the fair blowing on a whistle a Jew who was selling notions had given him.

He kept coming back to the carcasses of hogs, split and opened like great fleshy books, dripping with blood, which, pooled in the dirt, dogs risked kicks to lick. Pig kidney shaped like potatoes. Clumps of yellow fat. White salt pork.

Traif.

Intriguing.

Next to that booth, even more fascinating, was an old man—Michal Laski—whose bald head was as white and flaky as a mushroom's cap. His sheep-wool beard was yellow-stained, the tips where the hairs twirled together a darker, dirtier yellow.

According to rumors, Pan Michal came from a rich family. But he had married a woman—in some stories a whore, in others an aristocratic girl who had been ruined by a Russian officer—and had left his fortune, home, and family in Cracow.

His old coat—a nobleman's coat—was decorated with glass buttons. Inside each button was an insect: a blue-green fly, a bee, a tiny yellow moth. He was drinking vodka—and selling holy pictures, Christian saints and martyrs, with surprised eyes and gold halos as big and as solid as dinner plates. Gentile peasants, as they passed, took off their caps and crossed themselves.

And, here, among icons of St. Mark and St. Basil, St. Peter and St. Paul, St. Nicholas and St. Dumitry, the Holy Virgin and Mary Magdelene, Joseph paused.

He had a vague notion of Christianity—something about a dead man coming back to life, a false messiah. Other children had told him that gentile women even drank sacramental wine, which every Jewish boy knew would make a woman grow whiskers like men.

And he knew how dangerous it was to spend time with the *goyim*. But . . .

But Pan Michal told stories.

As he drank, occasionally selling an icon, often ignoring a prospective buyer, Pan Michal spun love stories—of Wanda and Rytogar, Walcerz and Heligunde—stories of vendettas like the battle between Wydzga and the Lodzinskis, war stories—of Casimir the Great and the Teutonic Knights . . .

Idling, half-hidden around the canvas corner of Pan Michal's booth, Joseph listened, rapt, to the old man just as his granddaughter Gittel would listen to her lover Solbetsky a hundred years later.

When Pan Michal told the story of Noah and the Flood, Joseph was surprised. *Noah!* It was like seeing a familiar face in a strange city.

After an hour or so, Pan Michal flicked a glance sideways at Joseph—but otherwise gave no indication that he had seen the boy, until night fell and Joseph drew nearer to the old man who smelled of woodsmoke, incense, and, very faintly, urine.

Pan Michal spoke softer and softer forcing Joseph to creep closer and closer—until Pan Michal snatched him.

"Who are you?" he muttered. "A Jew? A boy? What do you want? What are you doing hanging around?"

Joseph didn't answer. He struggled in Pan Michal's grip.

"Well," Pan Michal shrugged, "why not?"

He released Joseph, who, stumbling, ran through the muddy streets.

Almost home, Joseph slowed to a walk.

Across the road, the full moon cast parallel shadows of birches, making it look as if Joseph were climbing a ladder. A dark shape sailed in the corner of his eye. A hunting owl? A bat? Something was in Joseph's pocket, something Pan Michal had slipped in while he'd held Joseph.

From the pocket, Joseph took out a holy picture: a half-naked man, eyes rolled up to Heaven, holding his hands by his side, bleeding palms outward.

Joseph shuddered and threw the picture into the woods.

From that night on, whenever Joseph passed that spot in the road, he spit.

Weeks later, Joseph told Rose about what had happened.

Rose ran to the woods; but, no matter how hard she searched, she could not find the icon.

XIV

In mid-February, snow was banked as high as a man's shoulders. The drifts were black with soot from cooking fires. In the cold, the bare tree branches creaked like slow-moving wagons.

Joseph was walking through Plissa. A horse, suddenly raising and shaking its head, snorted, its nostrils half-clogged with ice. Joseph staggered back, almost falling. The horse lowered its head and trudged on.

Across the way, Joseph saw Pan Michal, drunk and half-frozen, lying on his side in the snow. His left—visible—cheek was marked with a silver spot of frostbite as if an old coin had been pressed into his flesh. Frozen spittle beaded his beard.

"Help," Pan Michal said. "Help."

Joseph glanced one way then the other. No one paid any attention to Pan Michal. No one stopped.

Pan Michal looked at Joseph. His eyes were red-rimmed, the whites as yellow as egg yolk.

"Help," he said, so softly Joseph wasn't even sure he'd really said it.

His heart beating wildly, confused by the sensation of sinning and doing a *mitzva* at the same time, Joseph pulled Pan Michal out of the snow.

The old man swayed above him, his shaggy black coat matted with ice. Then, Pan Michal grabbed Joseph's shoulder in a surprisingly strong grip, which Joseph couldn't break.

Pan Michal grinned at Joseph, his teeth black, his frostbitten cheeks pouching up, squeezing his eyes shut.

Giving Joseph a push, Pan Michal said, "This way."

Joseph had no choice but to lead the old man home.

Pan Michal's simple wooden house, built on a foundation of stacked, flat rocks, had an almost conical roof, missing shingles. The dirty snow by the door looked sculpted into gothic, deeply-etched but vague *bas reliefs* where Pan Michal had pissed. Inside the hut, a single chicken scratched in the filthy straw on the floor. Joseph gagged in the stench.

An ornate bedstead—carved with birds and rabbits hidden among wooden vines—dominated the single room. Nailed to the wall over the bed was a cross.

Joseph turned to run, but Pan Michal grabbed him.

"Fire," Pan Michal said.

Joseph tugged, trying to pull his shoulder from Pan Michal's grip. But the old man dug his gray fingers into Joseph's muscle, and, kicking the door closed with the heel of his boot, repeated, "Fire."

He shoved Joseph, who fell onto his knees near the filthy hearth.

"Fire," Pan Michal shouted.

Trembling, Joseph raked the few embers together and fed them twigs, the only kindling Pan Michal had inside the house. The fire caught.

Joseph looked around.

"There's no wood," he said.

Pan Michal grabbed the only chair, smashed it against the floor, then turned away from the splintered pieces, which Joseph put on the fire.

As Joseph worked, he glanced back at the old man, who rummaged in a cupboard for vodka. He found some and drank.

Pan Michal sighed and wiped his mouth.

"My wife," Pan Michal said, apologizing for the mess, "died."

It wasn't clear if she had died recently or a long time ago.

Pan Michal crossed himself.

Joseph started for the door.

"Wait," Pan Michal said, recognizing Joseph from the fair. "You're the boy who likes stories."

Joseph put his hand on the door latch.

"A *kaukas*—a dwarf—lives underground," Pan Michal said. "Under this house."

Joseph stopped.

"Just about where you're standing," Pan Michal said.

Joseph jumped aside.

Turning his back on the boy, Pan Michal slyly smiled.

"One night, the *kaukas* . . . ," Pan Michal started.

After telling Joseph the story of the *kaukas,* Pan Michal told the story of how the Sun and the Moon got married and had a child, Earth. How they quarreled and separated and could not decide who would keep the child, which they both loved; how they had to ask *Perkunas*, God of Thunder, who lives in a cloud castle and hunts demons—*pukys*—during storms; and how *Perkunas*, like Solomon, decided the Sun would watch over their child, Earth, by day and the Moon would watch over their child, Earth, by night.

"Zemyna—Mother Earth," Pan Michal chanted, *"from you I come, on you I live, to you I go."*

He drank more vodka.

"That's what *she"*—his wife—"used to pray every night," he said to Joseph, who, mesmerized, had edged closer to the old man, who told him how his wife had died two weeks earlier in a fever and how, at midnight, he could hear the click-clack of the paddle as her ghost churned blood into butter.

Pan Michal told more stories—*bigos,* a mishmash of Polish, Lithuanian, and Russian legends—about the unwise maid who washed her linen after sunset and how *Gabija,* the Fire God, dragged her by her long tresses into the Land of Flame where her hair turned red; about the wise maiden who attended to her spinning and ignored the handsome spirit who called out to her, *Lily and flax, lily and flax, come with me and be my wife*; about the Swan Maiden and the three princes; about the curious boy who found a he-goat as white as milk under a willow tree and climbed on its back and to this day cannot stop riding because the he-goat was *Slogute,* Nightmare; about the foolish young man who spurned the girl his father had chosen for him and instead wed a *laume,* a fairy, who used to stand under his window, her big fairy breasts bare in the moonlight . . .

"She was a perfect wife," Pan Michal said, as he set Joseph doing chores, sweeping, bringing split logs in from the woodpile, "and she gave him a perfect boy-child, and the young man was happy until one night he gazed on the fairy while she slept, and she melted into thin air."

The young man left his boy-child and, in despair, went

off to war, where he was killed. When his son was just Joseph's age, the boy set off to avenge his father's death, along the way strangling a *ragana*, a hag, who lived under a mountain, fighting a *milzinas*, a giant, and outwitting a *vilkolakis*, a werewolf, who had taken the form of a gentleman in a military uniform and who gambled with the boy by rolling the knucklebones of people he had eaten . . .

Pan Michal told stories—and drank vodka—until Joseph had finished the chores; then, Pan Michal crawled face down onto the bed and, snoring, fell into a drunken sleep.

Joseph stole out of the house and ran.

That night Joseph told Rose about his adventures; retold her all the stories, as Rose sat, wide-eyed, biting her lower lip; and confided that the *kaukas*—the dwarf—who lived under Pan Michal's house had, burrowing under the ground like a mole, followed Joseph all the way home.

XV

Three days later, Joseph came down with a fever— probably the same one that had killed Pan Michal's wife.

Heschel and Miriam wrapped Joseph up in a cloth and laid him on the shelf over the oven to sweat out the fever. They dabbed sugar water on his forehead, eyelids, and lips. They lit candles . . .

In the night, Rose crept to him.

Tell them about Pan Michal, she begged Joseph. *Tell them about the icon.*

No, Joseph said.

But he put a curse on you, Rose said, spitting as a precaution against the evil eye.

In the morning, as Joseph moaned and tossed, his eyes rolled up into his head, so he looked blind, Rose went to Pan Michal's house.

Pushing open the door, she found Pan Michal kneeling before the cross, praying.

She backed up two steps.

Pan Michal twisted his head around and glared over his shoulder at Rose.

"My brother . . . ," Rose said.

Pan Michal didn't say anything.

"He's sick," Rose said.

"What do you want from me?" Pan Michal asked.

"The curse," Rose said. "Take it off."

"Your brother . . . ," Pan Michal said. "He's the little Jew who was here?"

Rose nodded.

"And you think I put a curse on him," Pan Michal said.

Rose nodded.

Pan Michal turned back to the cross and gazed up at it for so long that Rose thought he'd forgotten about her.

At last, Pan Michal said, "I can't take off the curse."

Rose felt her eyes begin to burn with tears. Her brother's fever would get worse, and he would die.

"But," Pan Michal maliciously said, "*you* can."

"How?" Rose asked.

"Kneel beside me," Pan Michal said.

Rose did not move.

"You want your brother to get better?" Pan Michal asked.

"Yes," Rose said, softly.

Pan Michal nodded at a spot next to him. Slowly, Rose crossed the room and stood beside the old man.

"Kneel," Pan Michal said.

Feeling sick, Rose knelt.

"Do this," Pan Michal said, making the sign of the cross.

Rose hesitated.

"Do you want your brother to get better?" Pan Michal said.

Rose made the sign of the cross.

"Now," Pan Michal said, "repeat after me: *Pater noster . . .*"

Rose recited the *Our Father . . .* When she was done, she jumped up and ran from the house.

Pan Michal remained on his knees, but he had stopped praying. He dropped his eyes from the crucifix; and, for a long time, he just gazed at the wall.

By the time Rose got home, Joseph's fever had broken.

When Joseph recovered, Rose told him how she had cured him and made him swear never to tell their parents how she had sinned to save his life.

XVI

In 1756, when Joseph and Rose were sixteen years old, a holy man, Moritz Plaut—attended by nearly a hundred men, women, and children from other towns—came to Plissa with news of Jacob Frank, a Jew who, he said, would complete the mission initiated a century earlier by the false-Messiah Shabbati Zvi.

Shabbati Zvi—Plaut said—had been, not the true savior of the Jews, but the herald of the true savior, Frank.

Frank would conquer Christian and Turk, redeem Israel, rebuild the Temple, and usher in the End of Days, which was most assuredly coming. The signs were obvious. Rumors of war and famine. Hadn't there been the great earthquake in Portugal? A stone in a field near Warsaw had begun to bleed.

As Plaut's followers milled about outside the prayer house, singing holy songs, the men covering their eyes and dancing, most of the Jews from the village crowded inside the prayer house, where Plaut described how, within a year, the earth would become a Garden, where the Chosen would walk and discuss the Law in the cool of the day with the Patriarchs, Abraham, Isaac, and Jacob, with angels, with the Lord of Hosts, Himself, Blessed be He, God the Hidden, God the Absent . . .

Join me, Plaut urged, *in the New Path, the Way of Esau, a life of Perfect Freedom, beyond all Law except God's Love* . . .

Heschel the Newcomer, Yudel the baker, Meyer the cloth merchant and a dozen other men tried to protest, but their neighbors shouted them down and finally roughly shouldered them out of the door of the prayer house.

From inside, Heschel the Newcomer heard Plaut bellowing, *Join me, come with me to Kamieniec, where Jacob Frank will confront his enemies, the enemies of the Messiah, of the Lord of Hosts . . . Join me* . . .

That night, Joseph and Rose silently went about their chores, listening to their father argue with his friends: *What should they do about the madman Plaut, who spread*

*such terrible lies? What could they do about the madness that
had gripped Plissa?*

At the very moment Heschel the Newcomer and his
friends were meeting, dozens of villagers, convinced that
the Messianic Age was at hand, were giving away their
belongings, preparing to travel the next day—*the next
day!*—with the madman Plaut and his rabble to Kamieniec.

Joseph and Rose glanced at each other.

The Messianic Age . . . *Was* it about to begin? Could
they be *that* lucky? To be alive when the Gates of Wisdom
opened?

The earth would become a Garden, Plaut had promised,
*where the Chosen would walk and discuss the Law in the cool
of the day with the Patriarchs, Abraham, Isaac, and Jacob,
with angels, with the Lord of Hosts, Himself, Blessed be
He . . .*

Before dawn, Joseph and Rose stole out of their father's
house and joined the chanting, swaying, giddy crowd that
swarmed out of the village toward . . .

Toward what?

When Heschel the Newcomer learned that his children
had abandoned Plissa, abandoned the Faith of their Fathers, abandoned *him,* he ran out of his house and along the
road where Plaut had led the chanting and dancing crowd;
and, as he did when Bird had abducted Miriam, he fell to
his knees.

He beat his breast, shook his fists at the sky, and
demanded that *Hashem* explain why . . .

Why?

XVII

Two years passed.

Miriam died.

Heschel the Newcomer aged, it seemed, overnight. His hair went white. His eyesight dimmed.

At business, he was distracted. He spent hours praying, studying the Law, alone, ignoring the rumors of licentious behavior among Frank's followers; of bonfires fed with Torahs in Kamieniec, Lvov, Brody, and other towns; of Frank's flight to Turkey; of a mass baptism of five hundred— or was it five thousand?—Jews who had converted to Christianity.

Neglected, his house became so run-down that, on a summer morning, when Joseph unexpectedly returned, it reminded him of Pan Michal's house, which he had visited once as a child. From the shadows, where he rocked and prayed, Heschel the Newcomer blinked up at Joseph, this strange young man, as he stood, the sunlight so strong in the doorway behind him, Heschel the Newcomer could not make out his face.

Then, Heschel the Newcomer heard the cry of the baby that Joseph held in his arms.

At first, Heschel the Newcomer refused to believe this young man was his son. When Joseph had left Plissa, he'd been a youth. This stranger was too tall, too strong—a grown man.

But, by certain signs and the answers to questions Heschel the Newcomer asked, finally he was compelled to admit that, yes, this was his son—and that the child Joseph held was his grandson. Moses.

Who was the child's mother? When had Joseph married? What happened to Joseph's sister, Rose? Did they ever reach Kamieniec? What happened to Plaut?

Joseph did not answer his father. Or anyone else in Plissa who asked about the time he had been away.

Miriam's unmarried sister, Ruchel—Rachel—helped Joseph raise Moses until, a year after returning, Joseph married a widow, Ruth, with a son of her own, David.

The two boys—Moses and David—grew up inseparable. Moses, mischievous, like his father had been. David, cautious.

When Moses was four, Heschel the Newcomer happened to be walking along the riverbank when he saw Moses throwing stones at the branches of a pear tree, trying to knock down the ripe fruit. Heschel the Newcomer was about to call out, when he heard, behind the bushes to his right, the voice of his son, Joseph, who was talking to someone.

Why did Heschel the Newcomer approach softly so his son would not hear him? To eavesdrop? That doesn't seem in character for the pious, absent-minded old man Heschel the Newcomer had become.

Instinct? Premonition? Accident?

Whatever caused Heschel the Newcomer to approach so cautiously, he did—and he felt the skin on his scalp crawl as he realized from what Joseph was saying he was talking to Rose.

But where was Rose?

And what was he telling her?

She could rest in peace. Her child had grown up to be a strong, happy boy.

Rose was dead.

And Moses was her child, not Joseph's.

"Mine," Joseph said, when his father confronted him in the field.

"Your sister's," Heschel the Newcomer said, paradoxically proud of Joseph for trying to cover up for Rose's immorality.

"Mine," Joseph said.

"Your sister's," Heschel the Newcomer said.

"Mine," Joseph said. "Ours."

Incest!

To protect the child, Heschel the Newcomer agreed to keep the secret.

That afternoon, the old man took to his bed, where he stayed, talking to no one, not even going to the prayer house, for days.

One evening, a week or so after the confrontation with his father, Joseph returned home to find his son gone.

Where is Moses? Joseph asked.

Your father took him, Ruth said.

Uneasy, Joseph went to his father's house, which was empty. A woman returning from the fields told Joseph she had seen Heschel the Newcomer and Moses crossing the ford in the river beyond the orchard.

Joseph hurried to the ford, crossed the river, and followed a track, where, after a bit, he saw his father and his son—Heschel the Newcomer and Moses—laboring up a hill.

Heschel the Newcomer walked slowly, because of his failing health.

Moses walked slowly, because he carried a load of wood—just as Isaac had in the land of Moriah, when Abraham had taken him to be sacrificed for the Lord.

Sick with dread and relief, Joseph called out.

Moses stopped.

Heschel the Newcomer retraced his steps to meet Joseph, who saw in his father's girdle a large knife.

"What are you doing with my son?" Joseph asked his father.

"We are making a sin-offering to the Lord," Heschel the Newcomer said.

"And"—Joseph said, repeating the expected formula, as Heschel the Newcomer had done when he mistook the peddler for the Angel Gabriel—"where is the sheep for the burnt offering?"

"God will provide one," Heschel the Newcomer said.

"You're crazy," Joseph said.

"That's what Satan told Abraham," Heschel the Newcomer said, "to make him disobey Hashem."

"Give me the knife," Joseph said.

Heschel the Newcomer turned to go back to Moses, who stood a little way off.

"Give me the knife," Joseph repeated.

Heschel the Newcomer continued to walk toward Moses.

Joseph grabbed his father, who struggled in his grip, until Joseph seized the knife, which, in his rage, he turned on his father.

"Papa!" Moses cried to Joseph—who, shocked by what he was about to do and paralyzed by the sting of his multiple sins, dropped the knife and fell to his knees, covering his face with his hands.

Heschel the Newcomer picked up the knife, walked to Moses, who blinked at him with trusting eyes.

If Heschel the Newcomer had killed Moses, he would have been murdering as well all the following generations, including me.

Instead, Heschel the Newcomer broke the knife against a rock, choosing, not justice, but mercy.

Forgiveness.

Stop the music!

⤳ *epilogue*

Q. Why?

A. Why did mom go crazy?

Q. Why have you sifted her past, our family's past, trying to find out?

A. Why wouldn't I want to find out?

Q. I was wrong. You're not a goy. You're a Jew after all, answering a question with a question.

A. Why did you come when I conjured you?

Q. You didn't conjure me. The living are surrounded by ghosts. Usually, they ignore them.

A. Why can't I ignore you?

Q. Remember, every year on your birthday, how we used to wrestle?

A. Arm-wrestle.

Q. When you were eighteen, just before you went to college, you could have beat me. If you'd wanted to.

A. I was afraid . . .

Q. To win?

A. To have you lose.

Q. Why?

One generation passeth away, and another generation cometh; but the earth abideth for ever.

This is a fictional family history; and, like the family, some of the sources with their historical background and legends are invented. Those that are not include: various family oral histories, genealogical and historical records from the Leo Baeck Institute (New York), the Hall of Names at Yad Vashem: The Holocaust Martyrs' and Heroes' Remembrance Authority (Jerusalem, Israel), the Yivo Institute for Jewish Research (New York).

Other sources include:

The Dictionary of National Biography
The Encyclopedia Judaica
Jewish Daily Forward
New York Daily News
New York Mirror
New York Times

Providence Journal
Springfield Republican
Springfield Union
Elkan Nathan Adler, *Jewish Travelers in the Middle Ages*
Nathan Ausubel, *A Treasury of Jewish Folklore*
Yitzhak Baer, *A History of the Jews in Christian Spain*
Salo Wittmayer Baron, *A Social and Religious History of the Jews*
Willis Barnstone, *The Other Bible*
David Biale, *Eros and the Jews*
Emily D. Bilski, *Golem! Danger, Deliverance and Art*
Edward J. Bristow, *Prostitution and Prejudice: The Jewish Fight Against White Slavery, 1870–1939*
Eliyahu Ashtor, *The Jews of Moslem Spain*
Micha Joseph Bin Gorion, *Mimekor Yisrael: Classic Jewish Folktales*
William G. Braude, translation of Hayim Nahman Bialik and Yehoshua Hana Ravnitzky, *The Book of Legends: Sefer Ha-Aggadah*
Irving M. Bunim, *Ethics from Sinai*
James H. Charlsworth, *The Old Testament Pseudepigrapha*
A. Cohen, *Everyman's Talmud*
Israel Cohen, *Vilna*
Mark R. Cohen, translation of *The Autobiography of a Seventeenth-Century Venetian Rabbi: Leon Modena's Life of Judah*
Lucy S. Dawidowicz, *The Golden Tradition*
Nicholas de Lange, *Atlas of the Jewish World*
Yaffa Eliach, *Hasidic Tales of the Holocaust*
Perle Epstein, *Kabbalah: The Way of the Jewish Mystic*
James George Frazer, *Folk-lore in the Old Testament*

Moses Gaster, *Ma'aseh Book: Book of Jewish Tales and Legends Translated from the Judeo-German*

Louis Ginzberg, *Legends of the Jews*

Michael Gold, *Jews Without Money*

Robert Graves and Raphael Patai, *Hebrew Myths: The Book of Genesis*

Hutchins Hapgood, *The Spirit of the Ghetto*

Raul Hilberg, *The Destruction of the European Jews*

Irving Howe, *World of Our Fathers*

R. Po-Chia Hsia, *Trent 1475: Stories of a Ritual Murder Trial*

Frederic Huidekoper, *Judaism at Rome: B.C. 76 to A.D. 140*

Moshe Ideal, *Golem Jewish Magical and Mystical Traditions on the Artificial Anthropoid*

Moshe Idel, *Studies in Ecstatic Kabbalah*

Dan Jacobson, *The Story of the Stories: The Chosen People and Its God*

Paul Johnson, *A History of the Jews*

Jenna Weissman Joselit, *Our Gang: Jewish Crime and the New York Jewish Community, 1900–1940*

Rabbi Aryeh Kaplan, translation of Rabbi Yaakov Culi, *The Torah Anthology: MeAm Lo'ez*

Heszel Klepfisz, *Culture of Compassion: The Spirit of Polish Jewry from Hasidism to the Holocaust*

Hans Kung, *Judaism*

Samuel Kurinsky, *The Glassmakers: An Odyssey of the Jews*

Bentley Layton, translation of *The Gnostic Scriptures*

Waclaw Lednicki, *Life and Culture of Poland*

Raphael Mahler, *Hasidism and the Jewish Enlightenment*

Max L. Margolis and Alexander Marx, *A History of the Jewish People*

Joachim Neugroschel, *The Great Works of Jewish Fantasy and Occult*

Jacob Neusner, translation of *The Mishnah*

J. Noakes and G. Pridham, *Nazism: 1919–1945*

W.O.E. Oesterley and Theodore H. Robinson, *Hebrew Religion: Its Origin and Development*

Raphael Patai, *The Hebrew Goddess*

Raphael Patai, *The Jewish Mind*

Raphael Patai, *The Messiah Texts*

Arthur Rackwick, *Letters from the Crimean War, 1854–56*

Max Radin, *The Jews Among the Greeks and Romans*

Jacob S. Raisin, *Gentile Reactions to Jewish Ideals*

Angelo S. Rappoport, *Ancient Israel: Myths and Legends*

Rabbi A.B. Rhine, translation of Professor H. Graetz, *Popular History of the Jews*

Jacob Richman, *Laughs from Jewish Lore*

James M. Robinson, *The Nag Hammadi Library*

M.J. Rosman, *The Lord's Jews: Magnate-Jewish Relations in the Polish-Lithuanian Commonwealth during the 18th Century*

Cecil Roth, *History of the Jews*

Cecil Roth, *The Jews in the Renaissance*

David B. Ruderman, *Essential Papers on Jewish Culture in Renaissance and Baroque Italy*

Walter N. Sanning, *The Dissolution of Eastern European Jewry*

Rabbi Nosson Scherman, *Stone Edition of The Chumash*

Gershom G. Scholem, *Major Trends in Jewish Mysticism*

Gershom G. Scholem, *The Messianic Idea in Judaism*

Gershom G. Scholem, *On the Kabbalah and Its Symbolism*

Gershom G. Scholem, *Zohar: The Book of Splendor*

Bernard Schulman, *Shtarkes, Shnorrers, and Shlemiels: Marginal Jewish Life at the Turn of the Century*
Howard Schwartz, *Gabriel, Palace: Jewish Mystical Tales*
Howard Schwartz, *Lilith's Cave: Jewish Tales of the Supernatural*
William L. Shirer, *The Rise and Fall of the Third Reich*
Albert Speer, *Inside the Third Reich*
Adin Steinsaltz, *The Essential Talmud*
The Steinsaltz Edition of The Talmud
Victor Tcherikover, *Hellenistic Civilization and the Jews*
Joseph Tenenbaum, *Underground: The Story of a People*
Rita Thalmann and Emmanuel Feinermann, *Crystal Night*
Klaus Theweleit, *Male Fantasies*
Joshua Trachtenberg, *The Devil and the Jews*
Hugh Trevor-Roper, *Hitler's Table-Talk*
Rabbi Moshe Weissman, *The Midrash Says*
Leonard Wolf, translation of Beatrice Silverman Weinreich, *Yiddish Folktales*
Elie Wiesel, *Sages and Dreamers: Biblical, Talmudic, and Hasidic Portraits and Legends*
Robert Wilde, *The Treatment of the Jews in the Greek Christian Writers of the First Three Centuries*
Mark Zborowski and Elizabeth Herzog, *Life Is with People: The Jewish Little-Town of Eastern Europe*
Rabbi Meir Zlotowitz, translation of Bereishis: *Genesis*

COLOPHON

David Black is a scriptwriter, novelist, poet, journalist, and television producer. Among other honors, he has received the *Playboy* Best Article of the Year award and an Emmy nomination for "Law and Order." He has published nine books including *The King of Fifth Avenue* and *Like Father*, both *New York Times* Notable Books of the Year, and *The Plague Years* (about the AIDS epidemic), which was nominated for a Pulitzer Prize. He lives in New York City.

The text was set in Apollo, a typeface designed in 1964 by Adrian Frutiger (born in 1928), one of the most important type designers to emerge since World War II. The display face is Tema Cantante.

An Impossible Life was composed by Alabama Book Composition, Deatsville, Alabama. It was printed by Data Reproductions, Auburn Hills, Michigan on acid-free paper.